"What exactly d...

"Seducing you."

Damn. That was what Brody had been afraid of.

"You were trying to pretend we're just friends. Except we aren't," Genna murmured. "What we are is crazy attracted to each other. We need to act on that attraction…. The total act, with you naked. I'm willing to be on top if you're still holding on to that friendship myth of yours. That way you can tell yourself I took advantage."

He made some sort of choking sound, sure if he had any blood left in his brain it would have been words of protest.

Then Genna let her dress fall to the floor. Brody actually gulped trying not to swallow his tongue.

She was gorgeous.

Ivory limbs glowed like silk, the long sleek length of her interrupted by tiny pieces of black lace. He didn't know where to start. At the top, where the lace cupped the gentle slope of her breasts. Or at the bottom, where it was barely held in place by two tiny strings.

His gaze as hot as the blood rushing through his body, he decided to settle for the middle. At the cherry-red jewel decorating her belly button.

Screw friendship. And screw good sense.

He was gonna let Genna Reilly seduce him….

Blaze®

Dear Reader,

Aah, first love. For giddy teen Genna Reilly there's something extra exciting, and extra sweet, about that first rush of falling in love. She's so sure it's going to be perfect that she refuses to consider any other outcome. But Brody Lane knows better. Nothing in life is perfect, nothing ever turns out for the best, and love? He's pretty sure that's a fairy tale.

Still, one hot summer night, Genna's belief in love overcomes Brody's skepticism. Unfortunately, that first hot, sexy kiss results in the end of Genna's belief in perfection, and in Brody being shanghaied into the navy. But it doesn't end their feelings for each other.

Ten years later these two are still perfect for each other. But with so much baggage from the past, it's going to be difficult for them to face the very real challenges that the present brings. Brody is a navy SEAL wounded in duty. And Genna... well, Genna has a people-pleasing problem.

Genna and Brody were so fun to write. They just belonged together, and I loved telling their story. And since Brody and Genna's book is out in February, let me wish you happy Valentine's Day!

I hope you have a month filled with love and all things romantic, including some good books. Stop by my website, at www.tawnyweber.com, or visit me on Facebook and share your favorite Valentine memory. And look for my next Uniformly Hot! SEAL story, *A SEAL'S Kiss,* on sale in April 2014.

Cheers,

Tawny Weber

A SEAL's Salvation

—

Tawny Weber

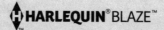

Recycling programs
for this product may
not exist in your area.

ISBN-13: 978-0-373-79787-5

A SEAL'S SALVATION

Copyright © 2014 by Tawny Weber

This is a work of fiction. Names, characters, places and incidents are either the product of the author's imagination or are used fictitiously, and any resemblance to actual persons, living or dead, business establishments, events or locales is entirely coincidental.

This edition published by arrangement with Harlequin Books S.A.

For questions and comments about the quality of this book, please contact us at CustomerService@Harlequin.com.

Printed in U.S.A.

ABOUT THE AUTHOR

USA TODAY bestselling author Tawny Weber has been writing sassy, sexy romances since her first Harlequin Blaze was published in 2007. A fan of Johnny Depp, cupcakes and color coordination, she spends a lot of her time shopping for cute shoes, scrapbooking and hanging out on Facebook.

Come by and visit her website, www.tawnyweber.com, for hunky contests, delicious recipes and lots of fun.

Books by Tawny Weber

HARLEQUIN BLAZE

COSMO RED-HOT READS FROM HARLEQUIN

To browse a current listing of all Tawny's titles, please visit www.Harlequin.com.

To Birgit.

Here's to many fabulous books.
I think we're going to have a lot of fun together!

_1_

Ten Years Before

"GENNA, YOU'RE CRAZY. You don't have to do this."

"Of course I do. You dared me." Genna Reilly gave her best friend a wide-eyed look. The one she used whenever she wanted to appear extra sweet and innocent.

The sweet part was usually an act. The innocent part was pure truth, though. But fingers crossed, tonight was going to change that.

"I didn't dare you. Dina did. You could just take the truth instead. C'mon, I'll even ask a different question," Macy said, her desperate tone matching the intense worry in her eyes. She grabbed both of Genna's hands, hanging on tight as if her body weight could anchor her to this spot. Since Genna was a lean, mean five-ten and Macy topped out at five-two, as anchors went, the girl wasn't very effective.

"That's not how the game is played," Genna said, carefully extricating her hands, not wanting to hurt Macy but desperately wanting to be gone already.

She'd had no idea tonight's slumber party would turn wild. Oh, sure, the potential was there. That's why they always had sleepovers at Dina's, because her mom fell asleep by ten and didn't do spot breathalyzer inspections like Genna's dad. It was easy to sneak out and do fun things. Like play truth or dare.

She'd figured on a fun weekend with three of her best friends, one of the last leading up to graduation. But she'd had no idea it would be this fun.

She needed to do this. Now, while the anticipation was still zinging through her system, making her feel brave enough to take on the world. Or, in this case, to take down the sexiest bad boy of Bedford, California.

She wanted Brody Lane.

But he had practically made a career of ignoring her existence.

Time to end that.

Class vice president, squad cheer captain and the daughter of one of the most influential men in town, at seventeen Genna was no stranger to attention. Her exotic looks, long silky black hair and sky-blue eyes ensured that she got plenty of male attention, and not only in her high school classes. Nope, even though they were three years her senior, her brother's friends were always staring and flirting with her, too.

But she wasn't interested in any of them.

Not the boys in school.

Not the guys her brother ran with.

Not until he'd started hanging out with Brody last winter.

For the first time in her charmed life, Genna was smitten. Hooked. Hot....

Over a guy who was deemed off-limits. Not only by her parents, who were ridiculously overprotective. But by the town itself, all of whom considered the Lanes just this side of the devil's minions, and Brody as a hell-raiser with an overdue ticket to prison. Heck, even her brother, Joe, had told her not to be stupid when he'd caught her checking out Brody's butt.

And Brody? He looked right through her as if she were made of cellophane. It wasn't as though she expected everyone in the world to adore her. But the guy could drool a little when he saw her in shorts, couldn't he? Or at least stare when he showed up to give Joe a ride and found Genna in a bikini, strategically washing her car.

But did he?

Noooo.

The guy acted as though she wasn't even there.

Genna wasn't the contrary sort. She'd never had to be. But no matter who told her or how many times, she couldn't get Brody Lane out of her head.

So tonight, thanks to Dina's dare, she was going to do something about it.

"Genna," Macy pleaded, as if she were peeking into her best friend's thoughts. "Don't do this."

"And be known as the girl who doesn't meet her dares?" She'd rather be known as an ax-murdering floozy who wore designer knockoffs and ugly shoes.

"Maybe Macy's right," Sylvie said quietly, always ready to jump in as the voice of reason. "This isn't like daring you to stand up in Mrs. Bellevue's class and sing 'The Star-Spangled Banner' while shaking your tail feathers. If your dad finds out, he'll kill you."

"He'll kill us," Macy intoned wisely, knowing full well that Sheriff Reilly was just as likely to punish any possible accomplices as he was the actual perpetrator.

"My dad's not going to find out," Genna said dismissively, the negligent wave of her hand stirring a tiny breeze in the sultry night air. Her father was too busy keeping the peace and freaking out over Joe's latest escapade to pay any attention to what his little angel did.

"I hear he's wild. He likes kinky stuff."

She assumed Dina was talking about Brody now and not her dad.

"What kind of kinky stuff?" Twisting her carefully streaked blond hair around one finger, Sylvie sounded somewhere between fascinated and terrified.

Genna wasn't between anything. She was smack-dab solid in determination. And feeling hot, of course.

"I dunno. But I'll bet Genna can tell us tomorrow." When Dina's loud giggle earned her three glares, she slapped both hands over her mouth. But she didn't stop laughing.

It was just nerves over being on the rougher side of town combined with a little too much hard lemonade. Or maybe she really thought it was funny that Genna was going to put all her virginal skills to use and seduce one of the baddest of the town's bad boys.

"I don't kiss and tell," Genna decided. That sounded mysterious, didn't it? And kinda sexy. Besides, she figured any kissing she did deserved to be savored. Which meant kept to herself, where the gossips and tattletales couldn't whisper it around.

"You mean you don't kiss or do anything else," Dina corrected, rolling her big blue eyes.

"Dina," Macy moaned, wringing her hands in a way that proved Genna's assertion that her friend took far too many drama classes. "Don't encourage her. She'll do something crazy."

"Oh, c'mon. It's not like she's really going to jump the guy," Dina retorted. As usual, she'd picked the scariest dare she could think of when they were playing. She'd had no idea it was also her friend's secret dream. "This is Genna. She's gonna go in there, because it's a dare and she can't resist those. She'll try to flirt, Luscious Lane will do his brick wall impersonation and it'll all be over."

"The dare was to kiss Brody Lane," Sylvie pointed out

quietly, casting a nervous glance toward the golden glow emanating from the garage light twenty feet away. "Genna's not going in there unless she's gonna follow through. You know that."

Genna stood a little straighter, her chin a smidge higher at that character evaluation. She liked being known as a girl who followed through.

She looked toward the garage, the silhouette of a man working on a motorcycle. Since Brody's dad, Brian, was working behind the counter and probably three-quarters to drunk at the bar next door, that meant it could only be his son in there.

Time to put up or shut up.

"If I'm not back in ten minutes, head home," she instructed, fluffing her hair and slicking a coat of Racy Red on her lips, then tucking the tube into the back pocket of her jeans. "I'll call you in the morning."

Before they could launch into warnings, cautions or any more stupid arguments, Genna hurried off. Her sandals made slapping sounds all the way to the garage like some kind of early-warning seduction device. She shot a quick glance back at her nervously huddled friends, then figuring that warning Brody wouldn't serve her plans, she slipped off her shoes.

Barefoot, she tiptoed up the last few feet of sidewalk and carefully peeked around the open doorway.

And there he was. Brody Lane, in all his bare-chested glory. Black hair, as stick-straight as her own, fell across his eyes as he bent over the Harley. Facing away from her, she had the perfect view of his denim-clad butt. And oh, what a butt it was. She wanted to touch it. She wanted to run her hands down the hard planes of his back, glowing gold in the poor garage lighting. Then she wanted to curl her fingers over those biceps. Rock-hard arms were so sexy in a guy, she decided then and there.

Genna fanned herself. Because, oh, baby, he was sizzling.

She took a deep breath, hoping it did intriguing things to her form. When a girl wasn't blessed with a whole lot on top, she learned these little tricks.

Then she stepped through the doorway.

She knew it was impossible given the distance, but she swore she heard a chorus of gasps from her friends. Not looking back, she stepped over the threshold, leaning her shoulder against the door frame; she rested one hand on her hip in a seductive pose she'd seen in a magazine.

And waited.

Nothing.

Genna rolled her eyes. Even when he didn't know she was there, he ignored her. This definitely had to change.

"Hey, Brody," she called out, relieved when her voice only shook a little. "How're you doing?"

His body went still; his head turned. His eyes, golden-brown like a cat's, narrowed.

Slowly, like a dream, he straightened away from the bike, the light glinting off that sleek golden skin. So, so much skin. Her gaze traveled from the broad stretch of his shoulders down his tapered waist to his jeans, slung low and loose on his hips.

Her mouth went dry. Oh, wow.

"Genna?" He cast a glance behind her, then back with an arched brow. "Joe isn't here."

She knew that. After the third screaming match with their father that week, her brother had torn off on his motorcycle before dinner, heading for the highway. To see one of his girls, Genna figured. Leaving the way clear for *her* to pay a visit to his best friend.

"I'm not here to see Joe."

Not the answer he'd been expecting, if his frown was anything to go by.

"Then what's up?" he asked, grabbing a rag and sliding the wrench through it before placing the tool in its spot in the big red toolbox. The area around him was as an oasis of tidy organization compared with the chaos of the rest of the garage. His space versus his dad's, Genna figured.

At her continued silence, he took a step closer, then stopped. She almost pouted. It was as if he'd heard a signal warning that she was there for something naughty.

"You have a problem with your BMW?" Frowning now, he gave her a quick once-over. Not in a sexy way, more as though he was worried she was hurt.

Genna's heart sighed. Wasn't he sweet?

"Nothing's wrong," she said, having to clear her throat after pushing the words through a mouth as dry as the Mojave. "So how're you doing? Is something wrong with your bike?"

It was all she could do not to wince at her own inanity. *Seriously, Genna? That's the best you can come up with?* She gave herself a mental slap upside the head as if it'd knock her back to normal. Normal Genna had no problem talking. And she'd spent the last three months practicing her flirting skills for an opportunity like this.

One where it was just her and Brody. Alone. Together.

Time to put all that practice to good use.

"You came to ask about my bike?"

"I came to visit with you," she corrected, taking another one of those deep breaths. His gaze didn't drop to her chest, though, so she let it out. No point hyperventilating. It wasn't going to make her breasts any bigger.

"Why?"

"Why not? You're a friend of my brother's. You're over at our place all the time." An exaggeration, since he'd been over maybe three times in the last year. Sheriff Reilly didn't care for troublemakers on his property. But that was beside the point. "You never visit with me, though. I figure it's because Joe's such an attention hog. My mom says he takes the title 'son' in the wrong way, figuring the whole universe revolves around him."

She grinned, waiting for him to join her. When he just stared, those gold eyes intent and cautious, she dimmed the smile a little. Obviously friendliness wasn't something he was overly familiar with. No point scaring him.

"And tonight I was out and about, and saw a light on." She gestured to the bulb swinging overhead with its halo of moths. "Since Joe's not around, I figured why not stop by and say hi."

"If Joe were here, you wouldn't have bothered?" He looked around, then spying the portable phone, grabbed it. To call her brother?

Genna's lips twitched. Wasn't he the gentleman? That's what was so fascinating about him, though. He didn't play the games boys her age did. From what she could tell, he didn't play games at all.

"Do you ever smile?" She wanted to see those lips turn upward and his gaze light up almost as much as she wanted to feel his mouth on hers and his eyes filled with desire.

He didn't respond. Just tucked his phone into his back pocket, crossed his arms over that sexy chest and stared.

"You gonna tell me why you're here? You lose a bet or something?"

Won a dare. But he didn't need to know that.

"I'll tell you as soon as you smile," she teased, stepping farther into the garage. She was hit with the scent of hot concrete, metal and oil she associated with car repair, and something else. Something earthy and appealing.

Soap. And man. Her belly quivered and her thighs trembled.

"Genna."

The sound of her name on his lips sent shivers through her, eliminating every niggling doubt or cautionary concern.

Leaving only excitement and desire.

"Actually, I'm here to seduce you," she blurted out. As if her words were gasoline on a fire, the already sultry air flared even hotter.

Good.

She was ready to get hot and wild.

SHIT.

Brody Lane had been in trouble plenty of times in his life. So many, it'd be easier to count the times he hadn't been in trouble.

But he'd never been as screwed as he was right now.

He was smart enough to know that.

What he wasn't was smart enough to know how to get himself out of it.

Genna Reilly.

Sugar-sweet and wickedly exotic.

The popular, preppy princess who got good grades, cheered at games and helped old ladies across the street.

About as opposite Brody's type as an eighty-year-old nun.

And the star of four out of five of his sexual fantasies.

A problem considering that at the tender age of seventeen, she was pure jailbait.

And so off-limits, she should be wrapped in barbed wire and sporting an alarm button.

Nobody messed with Sheriff Reilly's little girl.

Nobody.

And nobody'd have to be a total dumbass to not only cross that line, but to mess with Joe Reilly's little sister. The sheriff was a mean son of a bitch, but Joe was meaner. He didn't believe in letting a silly thing like the law get in his way.

Joe's mean side rarely bothered Brody.

Unless he was facing the possibility of having all that mean aimed his way.

Smart thinking said shoo Genna right back out of his garage and out to the very edges of his life again. The edge where she only showed up on the opposite side of the street from time to time. And in his hot, sweaty dreams every night.

"Are you gonna offer me a beer?" she asked, tilting her head toward the six-pack minus one he'd left in the cooler.

"You're underage."

Eyes rounded in amusement, she gestured to the one he'd cracked open an hour ago, then forgot about after one swig.

"Pot, meet kettle?"

Brody's lips twitched. Damn, she had a smart mouth.

A very sexy, pouty-lipped smart mouth.

One he spent way too much time fantasizing over.

One he'd worked damned hard to ignore.

"I'm not aiding and abetting underage drinking," he said with a shrug. He didn't mind the hypocrite label. He'd sported worse. And he didn't think Genna, with any fewer inhibitions than she had already, was good for his peace of mind.

"So why are you here again?" he asked with his darkest glower. "Because we both know you're not the seducing kind."

He wanted to shove her out the door. Except that'd require touching her. So maybe he could mean her out instead. It always worked for his old man. The guy opened his nasty mouth and cleared a room in less than a minute.

"Why am I here?" she repeated, clearly buying time as she wet her lips and took a nervous breath. The move sent the ruffles of her halter fluttering in a way Brody had no business noticing. "I'm here because of a dare."

Figured. Brody crossed his arms over his chest.

"You're here to use me?"

Her lower lip dropped, then jutted out in a pout. He didn't figure she had the experience to realize just how freaking sexy that move was.

He did, though.

His rapidly hardening dick echoed its agreement.

"I wouldn't use you."

"No? So you came in here to talk to the bad boy of Bedford because you were craving my scintillating conversation?"

She started to giggle, then pressed her lips together, her face so amused she looked as if she were going to burst at any second.

"What?" he prodded with a growl.

"You said scintillating."

"Yeah? So? I know how to read, too." Damn, he hated this town. Everyone—even the sexy wannabe seductress in front of him—thought they had him so figured out. Labeled and dismissed, they never looked past his last name.

Hell, Genna's own brother, Joe, was way worse than Brody when it came to trouble. But people looked at his Harley, a brand-new, off-the-showroom-floor graduation gift, and smiled. They looked at Brody's, bought after years of scrubbing dishes in the back of the bar, pumping gas and wrenching at Lou's Garage, and saw trouble.

"I didn't mean to suggest you were stupid," Genna said with honest bluntness, her expression somewhere between indignant and horrified. "I just think it's a funny word."

"Right."

"I do. Like grandiose." Brody grinned at the way she seemed to relish the word, drawing it out in a tone worthy of a royal princess.

"You like things really big?" he mused before he could stop himself.

Her eyes lit, the worry leaving her face and her smile

returning like a ray of sunlight. It made him want to smile back. Almost.

"Participle?" She offered the word like a hostess offering a drink. As if inviting him to indulge.

"Does it dangle?"

Her laugh gurgled out, about the lightest, happiest sound to ever ring through this murky garage.

Brody couldn't help himself. He grinned. He just had to.

"You're cute," she decided, still smiling.

"Yeah?" He'd never been called cute before. Any number of other four-letter words, but not that one.

"Yeah," she said, stepping closer. Too close. Her scent wrapped around him, light and tasty, like the daiquiris he mixed in the bar on nights his old man passed out before closing.

Brody's smile disappeared.

Shit. She thought they were having a conversation.

He should have stuck to grumpy and silent.

"You need to leave."

Please.

"I don't think so," she murmured, her words so quiet they were a whisper on the heavy night air.

He could actually feel his brains start to slip away. Bad news, since he needed them. They were there to remind him to stay away from her. To caution him to keep his hands to himself. To warn him about those male relatives of hers. The ones he was supposed to watch out for. Whatever the hell their names were.

But she was close enough now for him to see the band of midnight encircling her pupils, all the more vivid against the pale blue of her irises.

"You really need to go." Desperate, he reached out to move her aside. Because if she wasn't leaving, he was.

But the minute he touched her, all thought of either one of them leaving fled. His fingers curled over the smooth, deliciously soft skin of her upper arms. She was so slender, but he could feel the muscles there. She was so warm, he felt like a tiny piece of him, forever frozen, was melting in his chest.

It was terrifying.

Those fascinating eyes huge and locked on his, she reached out to trail her fingers over his chest. Her touch was so soft and tentative, as if she were petting a wild animal. Or a rabid dog.

Brody wondered if he bared his teeth and growled, would she run?

He should try it.

But those fingers had shorted out his ability to think.

It was as if she'd reached in and flipped the last switch.

Brain, off.

Dick, on.

When she leaned closer, he realized she was the perfect height.

She fit perfectly against his body, her slender curves hitting all his favorite spots.

Her mouth was right there. Waiting.

He dropped his gaze, noting the slight quiver in the full, red cushion of her lower lip. He met her eyes again. No nerves there. Just heat. Pure, hot, intense.

Insistent.

"Kiss me."

"It's a bad idea."

"Sure it is," she agreed, her gaze not leaving his as she leaned in, closing those last few infinitesimal inches between them. Her breath warmed his mouth just before she brushed the slightest whisper of a kiss against his lips.

"So be bad."

2

GENNA'S ENTIRE BODY was quivering. Nerves. Excitement. Desire. She couldn't tell which was which. Just knew they were all there.

She stared up at Brody, her entire being engulfed by his presence. Everything was brighter. Stronger. Bigger.

The overhead light glinted blue in the vivid black of his hair as it fell over his forehead, stick-straight strands hanging in his golden-brown eyes.

Her heart beat so hard against her chest she was surprised it didn't jump right out and glom on to him. She wanted him so much. Breathing deeply, she filled her lungs with his scent. Clean like soap, but earthy. All male. All man.

Her lips trembled so much, she wanted to bite down to keep them still. But she was afraid that might discourage him from taking her *be bad* suggestion.

She really wanted him to be bad.

She needed him to take over. Because that kiss, that tiny little brush of her lips, that was about the extent of her experience.

"Please," she whispered.

Ah, there it was. The magic word. Brody closed his

eyes as if in prayer. When he opened them, the caution was gone. Instead, he was looking at her as though he was starving. As though he was the big bad wolf, and she was a delicious treat.

His gaze locked on hers, demanding that she watch him kiss her.

His lips were so soft. Tension she hadn't allowed herself to acknowledge seeped away as they rubbed over hers. Angling this way, shaping her mouth that way. So wonderful.

Then his tongue slid over the seam of her lips. Wet heat.

Oops, there came that tension again. And it'd brought a whole slew of wickedly enticing feelings with it. They whipped through her body, making her knees weak. Her heart race. And her panties damp.

His lips were just a whisper against hers. Still soft as he seemed to be memorizing the shape of her mouth with his tongue. He was touching only her shoulders, his hands so light she could barely feel them.

But the look in his eyes was so intense, so demanding, that she shivered. It was as if he were promising that she'd have to strip naked and share her every naughty secret. That she do all sorts of things she'd only heard in whispers, read in her favorite romance novels and sneaked peeks at on the internet.

She'd never realized that fear had a sexy edge. That the aching physical lure of it could beckon, even as her mind cautioned her that this kiss, this man, and whatever was coming next, were way, way out of her league.

Then, as if he couldn't stand the teasing any longer, his tongue swept into her mouth and, thankfully, his eyes closed. Releasing her.

He tasted so good. His tongue was pure power as it slid along hers, teaching her how he wanted her to respond.

Genna moaned, her stomach feeling as if she'd just taken a dive on a roller coaster.

Relieved, she closed her own eyes, concentrating instead on the clamoring of sensations spinning through her body. It was easier this way. It felt safer. As though she could just let go and not worry about what might happen next.

Her hands trailed, whisper-soft, over his chest. He was so hard, muscled but not bulky. Her fingers found a scar, long and rigid. As she wrapped her arms low around his back, she discovered a few more. She wanted to kiss them, every single one. To wish away the hurts she knew he'd suffered. She wanted to make him happy. To make him feel so good, he'd forget about all the bad he'd ever felt.

As if hearing her wish, her fingers—and she swore it was of their own volition—skimmed the waistband of his jeans. The fabric was soft. Worn. And so easy to slip her hand beneath.

His breath caught, the action pressing his hard chest against her aching nipples. He groaned, a low rumble against her mouth, before pulling away.

She wasn't sure, since her blood was pounding too hard for her to hear, but she thought she whimpered.

"No."

"Yes," she whispered back. She wanted to smile, to marshal together a clever argument that'd convince him that this was a good idea. But deep inside, beneath the crush that was driving her past reason, she knew it really wasn't. Just as she knew he wasn't going to listen to a thing she said.

Which left only one option for getting her way.

And that was physical.

More nervous than before her driving test, her SATs and opening her letter from Stanford combined, Genna took a deep breath to calm the dragons dancing in her stomach and leaned back a little. Not enough to put any real distance between her and Brody. Definitely not enough to give him the silly idea that they might be done here. But enough for her to reach up, sliding her hands under the heavy curtain of her hair. Her fingers quickly picked apart the bow tying her halter behind her neck.

His eyes wide and worried, Brody shook his head as if he could deny what she was about to do. But he didn't stop her. Instead, his gaze dropped, watching first her hands, and then the fabric of her blouse, drop to her waist.

Genna bit her lip to stop their trembling.

And waited.

His eyes weren't worried now. They were hot. Hot and intense and greedy.

His lids lowered, but didn't hide the sensual gleam. She could see the pulse beating, fast and furious, in his throat. He looked as if he could eat her up in one big, juicy bite.

So why didn't he?

She'd heard that sexual frustration was a bad thing, but she didn't think it was supposed to come with a big fat dose of anger.

Wasn't he supposed to do *something?* Be so overcome by lust that he grabbed her and took all the choices and moves and decisions out of her hands? That's how it happened in all the books. Clearly, he needed to read more.

"If you don't do something, I'm gonna kick you," she told him through gritted teeth.

"Baby, this is wrong."

Genna melted. The way he said baby, sort of low and growly, was so sexy and sweet.

"Then show me how to do it right."

He gave a laughing sort of groan. It was the first time she'd seen him laugh, she realized. The first time she'd been close enough to watch how it made his eyes light, his face look younger. Softer.

Sweeter.

"Don't you want to touch me?" Taking his hand in hers,

she lifted it to her bare breast. His palm was like fire on her skin. Her nipple tightened to an aching point, shooting a swirling shaft of desire straight down to settle between her thighs.

His pupils were so big, they made his eyes look pitch-black. His face was sharp in the shadows. She swallowed hard, wanting to ask if it felt as good to him as it did to her, but afraid to say a word.

Then he stepped closer. His body, hot and damp in the sultry night air, heated hers. A bead of sweat trickled down Genna's spine.

Eyes huge, nervous, she watched and waited.

As if he was moving in slow motion, Brody leaned forward, his hair sweeping down to curtain his face in black silk. It was so soft as it slid against her skin. Then he took her nipple into his mouth.

Hot and wet.

His lips brushed, his tongue swirled. Then he scraped the edge of his teeth over the aching bud.

Genna cried out, her fingers clutching his shoulders.

Brody sucked harder, his long, sure fingers pressed against the seam of her jeans. Need unlike anything she'd ever felt, more than anything she'd ever imagined, gripped her. Not sure what she was doing, how to quench the tightening demand of her body, Genna swiveled her hips in slow circles against his hand. Her fingers dug into the waistband of his jeans. Then, desperate to feel him, even as she hoped he'd take it as a hint to do the same, she unsnapped his jeans.

Lightning fast, Brody's hand grabbed hers and his head shot up.

It was like being speared by gold light, his eyes were so fierce. Nerves joined desire to swirl in an uncomfortable dance in her belly.

Genna bit her lip, waiting.

Was he going to stop?

Did she want him to?

Before she could decide, before she could even identify all the feelings bombarding her, he swept her into his arms.

Oh, God. Genna melted, body, heart and all, as he carried her three steps to an old bench-style car seat leaning against the wall.

It was so romantic.

They fell together onto the ratty black surface, with her on Brody's lap. He immediately rolled so she was underneath him. His mouth took hers again. This time it was harder. More demanding. He wouldn't let her play passive. He wanted everything she had to offer.

As soon as her tongue ventured out, sliding into his mouth, he rewarded her by cupping his hand over her bare breast again.

She flew higher. His fingers plucked at her nipple. She swirled, stars crowding the edges of her vision. She mewed in protest when his hand left her breast, then purred as it cruised down to her jeans. Her heart stopped, waiting for him to unsnap the denim.

He slipped right past the zipper though, again, pressing tight against her aching core through her pants. The heel of his hand rotated and his nails scraped.

Breath ragged, Genna tried to figure out what was happening to her body. It kept getting tighter and tighter, curling around and around, spinning out of control.

His mouth, so hot and wet on her nipple, moved away. She gasped when he blew on the wet flesh. Then he bit down.

And she exploded.

Lights flashed behind her eyes. Her pants were whimpers now. Her body on fire. She arched against his hand, wanting more. Needing more. Her thighs pulsated, the flesh between them throbbing.

"More," she murmured as she floated back to earth.

She slid her fingers into his hair, scooping it back off his face. He looked like one of those fallen angels. Too gorgeous to be real, too tempting to resist.

"I want more," she said again. "I want everything."

Brody looked as if he was at war with himself.

Before she could find out which side won, though, there was a loud racket by the door.

"Lane? Brody Lane? You here?"

Genna jumped so high, she was pretty sure she bruised her ass when she landed.

Passion fled so fast, it was as if it'd never existed. Panic gripped her belly in a greasy, vicious twist, making her want to whimper. She didn't have to look toward the door to know who was yelling. She'd heard that voice every day of her life.

Ohmygod. She was so dead.

They were off in the corner, out of view of the door. Were they hidden enough? Maybe if they didn't move, he'd go away.

Her eyes, wide and blurred by a haze of terror, met Brody's. His face, so soft and sweet and passionate only moments before, was like granite now. His lips pressed tight, his eyes chips of gold. He looked scary. As though he was taking that threat seriously and about to go to battle for his life.

Genna wanted to reassure him, to say it'd all be okay. That this wasn't going to be as bad as whatever he was imagining. But she was a lousy liar.

And that hadn't been an idle threat.

And she was pretty sure whatever he was imagining had nothing on the reality.

'Cause they were seriously dead.

When the knots in her stomach did a sickening lurch from side to side, she closed her eyes and breathed through clenched teeth and prayed she wouldn't puke all over Brody. Not that he was ever going to want to talk to her again after this. But still, that's hardly the last impression a girl wanted to make on the guy who'd given her her first orgasm just before her father killed him.

Maybe if they stayed here, didn't move, it'd all go away. Like the bad dreams she still had every once in a while. She just lay there, eyes closed, and waited.

The silence was broken by the sound of a shotgun chambering a round.

Genna gulped.

Waiting was probably out of the question.

Clearly in agreement with her brilliant assessment, Brody shifted. He didn't wait for her to pull up her top, instead yanking the halter so high she was afraid it'd end up tied around her mouth.

Taking her cue, she reached behind her and tried, three times, to tie it. Finally she managed some sort of knot that included a lot of her hair and a broken fingernail.

As soon as her fingers cleared the knot, he stood. If she'd had a voice, she'd protest his hurry. Didn't the guy know it was always better to put off ugly confrontations?

Genna stared at the hand he held out. The long fingers that, only minutes ago, had been teaching her what pleasure really was. At his impatient look, she grimaced and took his hand. He pulled so hard, she almost flew to her feet.

Midflight, she got a look at her father standing in the doorway.

Holy hell.

She tried to swallow, but couldn't get any spit past the knot of terror in her throat.

Her entire body started shaking, but this time she knew it was pure fear. Knowing it was insane to touch Brody, but needing the support all the same because her knees had just turned to water, she gripped the back of his jeans, the fabric still slack thanks to her quick work with his zipper.

"Hi, Daddy," she said, not at all sure he wouldn't pull the trigger.

FOR JUST A BRIEF, blissful few minutes, Brody had come as close to happy as he'd ever been in his life. Heaven couldn't feel as good as Genna Reilly did in his arms. And heaven, like Genna, was obviously not available to guys like him.

He should have known better. Hell, he had known better. Brody had to wonder when he'd finally learn. Anytime something looked too good to be true, it was. And a girl like Genna, she was not only too good to be true, she was so far off-limits that he was only surprised her cop father hadn't shown up earlier. The guy had to have a warning alarm planted on her somewhere. Brody just wasn't sure what'd triggered it. His hands on her body, or his lips on her mouth.

And it totally pissed him off that he considered both worth whatever price he was about to pay.

Teeth clenched, he eyed the shotgun. It was gonna be one helluva price, too.

"I'm gonna kick your ass," Sheriff Reilly growled, fury radiating off the guy in waves.

Brody braced, feet planted firm and fists loose at his side. His body was wired tight, ready to dive to either side. He'd spent most of his life facing one attack or another. He figured at least he'd earned this one.

He didn't wait long. The sheriff was on him in a flash. The guy was a lot faster, and in better shape, than Brody's old man. They flew backward, trapping Brody against the wall right next to where Genna had stripped down and blown his mind.

"Daddy!" Genna jumped forward, grabbing on to her father's arm and tugging. She was a tall girl, but as slight as a wish and no match for her muscular father when he shook her off. She fell backward, stumbling over Brody's bike and sending the Harley crashing to the floor. It barely slowed her down, though. She was back and grabbing on her father, tugging and demanding that he let Brody go.

Apparently unable to effectively threaten and deal with his daughter at the same time, the sheriff spun with a roar, grabbed his daughter by the shoulder, swept the shotgun off the floor where he'd thrown it before his dive. He shoved Genna toward the door.

"Get the hell in the car, Genna Yvonne. Now. I'll deal with you later."

"You're not going to hurt Brody. You can't. He didn't do anything." Tears soaked her cheeks, but Genna didn't budge from her position between her father and Brody.

"Don't you dare tell me what I'm going to do," her father growled, his face contorted in fury.

The cop raised his fist in the same move he'd pulled on Brody. Would he follow through? Rumor was that Genna was a pampered princess. Joe would have gladly outed his old man if the guy hit her.

Still…

"Don't."

That's all Brody said. He wasn't getting in the middle of family drama. He'd spent enough time in his own to know that bystanders were safer on the sidelines, and participants never appreciated interference. But he'd be damned if the guy was gonna get violent with Genna. Not in front of Brody, not later in private, not ever.

"Shut your mouth and sit down, Lane," the sheriff barked, confirming Brody's take on bystander interference. "I'll deal with you in a minute."

"There's nothing to deal with. I didn't break any laws, you have no reasonable cause to be here and this is private property," Brody pointed out quietly.

"You were in here with my daughter."

"When did a kiss become illegal?"

"When she's my daughter," Reilly growled, lunging again. Brody grimaced, knowing this time the guy was going for more than intimidation.

"Daddy! Stop or I'll call 911."

Genna's horrified cry was like a bucket of water over the man's head. It only took a blink for the rage to clear from his eyes and the cop-face to fall back into place. Brody didn't take a lot of comfort from that. He'd been kicked around plenty by cops wearing that same neutral look. But he wasn't worried about getting shot any longer.

"You touched my daughter."

Expressionless, Brody returned the dead-eyed stare, but didn't say anything. Why bother? The sheriff had walked in on them together. Lying was pointless and admitting it was probably admissible in the ass-kicking court the guy was convening.

The tension in the room seemed to ratchet up to the point that even Brody was shifting uncomfortably. He hated inaction. Kick his ass or get the hell out already. He managed—barely—to keep that suggestion to himself, though.

Finally, Reilly gave a grunt. He shouldered the shotgun, took his cuffs from his belt and gestured with his chin for Brody to turn around.

"You arresting me?"

Reilly's gaze shifted from Brody to Genna, then to the bottle of beer on the workbench.

"We'll discuss it." He lifted his hands, the cuffs dangling from one finger. "Turn around."

More intimidation. He had nothing. The beer was warm enough by now that it could have been Brian's, left there before the old man had gone to work his shift in the bar. Getting hot and heavy with Genna was stupid, but not a criminal offense. Fine. Brody sighed, then turned around. Let the guy cuff him and play hard-ass.

"Dad—"

"You say another word and it'll be on his tab," Reilly warned Genna, his icy glare making it clear the bill was already more than Brody could afford.

Whatever.

"Let it go," Brody murmured. Not that he expected her to take his advice. Hell, they didn't even know each other. But there was no point in her making it worse for either of them. Let it go and move on, was Brody's motto.

"I'll be right back," the man promised, giving the cuffs a smack that ricocheted painfully through Brody's arms.

"I'll be here."

Shifting his shoulders, trying to find an angle that didn't hurt like a son of a bitch since the guy had hooked the cuffs around the steel grip on a huge toolbox. To, what? Keep him from running away? Brody silently cussed up a storm and watched Reilly drag his daughter out of the garage.

The last sight Brody had of Genna was the tear-filled apology in those big blue eyes.

Damn, she was pretty.

He should regret it.

She wasn't his type, and she came with an insanely high price tag.

But the sweet taste of Genna was still on his lips. His fingers still tingled with the memory of her silky skin, the soft weight of her hair. Yeah. She was a mistake. But, even as he shifted again trying to ease the pressure on his shoulders, he couldn't regret making it.

"Took your time," he snapped when Sheriff Reilly sauntered back into the garage. Thankfully without the shotgun this time. He didn't look any happier, though.

"You in a hurry?"

"I have things to do." More importantly, he'd like to get

this over before the old man was off shift. Nothing pissed him off more than hearing Brody had been in yet another scrape with the law.

"You're gonna have to reschedule."

"Why? You're seriously hauling me in?" Brody wanted to laugh. Another black mark on his record wasn't going hurt, but it was gonna irritate. Worse, it was going to disappoint his gramma. And he'd been trying hard the last few years to stop doing that. Irene Lane had this crazy belief that Brody could build a good life. Could be the kind of guy she could tell her friends about, could brag on and be proud of.

"I figure there's only one answer to this little problem you've presented me with tonight."

His expression bored, Brody arched one brow in question.

"You'll have to leave Bedford."

Hell, yeah. It was like the guy had poked into Brody's brain and picked out his secret dream. Still…

"You can't kick me out of town."

"Boy, I can do whatever I damned well please."

Brody considered a testament to his control that he didn't roll his eyes. Because they both knew the guy was claiming powers he didn't have.

"Let's see. I've got you on underage drinking. Driving on a suspended. That fight last week with the Kinski boys, I'll bet they'd file charges if pressed. I can call that aggravated assault. Your bike has modified pipes, violating the sound laws." He went on reciting his list of minor offenses, boring the hell out of Brody. Was that the best he had?

Clearly reading his disdain, the sheriff shifted gears.

"You're a bad influence on Joe, and I know you're both involved in gang activity. I can make your life hell figuring out which gang, and what you're doing. Or I can put the word out that you're playing nice with me and let the gangs take care of you."

That caused a twinge, but Brody shrugged it off. He was clean and gang-free, but his friend wasn't. Still, Joe was a big boy. He knew what he was getting into.

"So that's all you got?" Brody asked, his laugh just this side of a sneer. "A handful of petty offenses and a few threats?"

Reilly stared. Just stared. For so long, Brody's neck itched and he wanted to squirm.

"Son, you're getting the hell out of here one way or another.

Hell yeah, he was. He'd spent the last four years saving up, cleaning up and getting his act together so he could see the end of Bedford.

Three more months.

That's all he needed to have enough cash to pay back the last of what his gramma had spent bailing him out of juvie, paying a lawyer to seal his records and covering his hospital bills. She'd mortgaged her house for him, and when he'd promised to pay it off himself, she'd doubled down with guilt, demanding he stay in town until it was paid. Her way, he knew, of watching over him as long as she could. She'd tried to get him to move in with her, but they both knew that was a bad idea. The few times he'd lived with her, Brian inevitably showed up, remembered he had a mother who might have some money and happily pounded on both of them. So Brody made a point to do as little as possible to remind the old man of Irene's existence.

But he hadn't been able to ignore her plea that he stay in town. The minute his slate was clean, he was outta there.

And never coming back.

"I'll be gone soon enough," Brody said. Then, pissed that he sounded weak, as if he were giving in to cop intimidation, he pulled out his best sneer. "You don't have to worry about your pretty little girl. I promise I'll keep my hands off her between now and then. No guarantees that she'll reciprocate, though."

Brody instantly regretted his words. He had no issue taunting the cop. But waving Genna around like that was cheap. Wrong.

And clearly the equivalent of a red flag in front of a charging bull.

Sheriff Reilly went from calm cop to furious father in an instant. His eyes, the same blue as Genna's, Brody realized with an audible gulp, narrowed into slits. His fists clenched, then as if making sure he hadn't broken any of his own bones, he slowly flexed his fingers before wrapping one hand over the butt of his gun. The sound of the release tab loosening was like fingernails on a chalkboard. Loud, painful and threatening.

Brody had spent the first half of his life a punching bag, the convenient focal point for every frustration, irritation or random violent thought his old man had entertained. He'd spent two idiotic years on the streets, honing his fighting skills and learning just how viciously painful a knife in the gut was.

But he'd never been scared for his life the way he was now.

"You won't hurt me," he said with his usual cocky assurance, even though he was nothing but. "You're not gonna risk your badge, or your self-respect, breaking those laws you love so much."

At least, Brody hoped he wasn't. Because Sheriff Reilly looked furious enough to kick his ass inside out, then rip the pieces to shreds.

And then the guy pulled it all in. Brody had to admire that, the way he could control all that fury, channel his emotions. It was seriously impressive. And not because it meant Brody wasn't gonna get beat up.

"As I see it, I have a couple choices," the sheriff mused in a cool tone. "I can do just what you said, and accept the results of those risks. Or I can make sure you get outta here."

"And I have no choice in leaving?"

"Actually, you do have a choice. You can choose army or navy. But that's about as much say as you're gonna get in this."

Brody laughed. There wasn't a damned thing funny in the sheriff's expression, but that had to be a joke. The guy could toss him in jail; he could probably get away with kicking his ass. But he couldn't force him to join the military.

"I'm not soldier material."

The sheriff smiled his agreement. "You're gonna be."

"Or?"

Reilly nodded, clearly pleased that Brody saw the reality. This was definitely an either-or situation.

"Or I haul your ass in on statutory rape charges. Genna's seventeen."

"We didn't—" Brody bit the words off, not about to share details of just what they had and hadn't done. "I didn't rape your daughter."

"Legal semantics," Reilly mused. "Statutory rape might not denote force, but that word, it's a lightning rod. And a case like this, the town bad boy and a straight-A student, a vulnerable girl whose life is now ruined? That'll make the news. Throw in your record, your rumored gang affiliation? I'll bet this goes national. Won't that be interesting? All that attention here on Bedford. Bet your gramma will be bursting with pride. She got anything left to sell off to pay legal fees?"

Brody swore a blue streak, yanking out every cussword and vile epithet he knew. The cop didn't blink.

By most accounts, Sheriff Reilly was a fair cop. He

cozied up tight to the letter of the law and prided himself on his position in town. But Joe had said more than once that his old man was a prick who cared more about appearances, about that precious rep of his, than he did his family. That he'd do anything to keep their reputation as shiny bright as he did his badge.

But Brody couldn't believe that included punishing his daughter with public humiliation.

Or maybe he just didn't want to believe it.

But shock didn't blunt his anger. He'd done a lot of shit in his life that probably deserved punishment. But not tonight. Not like this.

His gramma didn't hold out a lot of hope that her family would meet any decent standards. But having her grandson branded a rapist would pretty much kill her.

Genna would be publicly humiliated, dragged through the drama of a court hearing. She'd have to face reporters and gossips and nastiness in the form of support. Brody had seen plenty of that over the years, the gleeful joy others took in their hypocritical sympathy.

Numb, as if the fury had pounded itself out against his temples, he met Reilly's eyes. Brody wasn't a poker player, but he was the product of violence. He knew absolute determination when it stared back at him.

If he didn't fall in line, he'd pay.

And he was fine with that.

But Genna and Gramma Irene would pay, too.

Trapped, Brody quit struggling against the cuffs. His shoulders sank low and for the first time in his life, he felt defeated.

He vowed then and there that this was the last time he would ever let his dick get him in trouble.

3

The Present

"YOU BLOW MY MIND, DUDE. We've been on this aircraft carrier for what? All of a day and you're already making trouble?"

"Trouble? Dude, that wasn't trouble. Believe me, I know the difference." Petty Officer First Class Brody Lane, call sign Bad Ass, dropped to his rack with a grin, folding his hands behind his head and crossing his booted ankles.

"Farm Boy said some wet-behind-the-ears recruit threatened to kick your ass." Masters gestured to their teammate who'd returned from the poker game a few minutes before Brody.

Their SEAL team had hitched a ride on a navy aircraft carrier on their way back from a training mission. And while they weren't treated as dignitaries as they crossed the Atlantic, they were given a ten-man berthing area to use instead of having to bunk with the rest of the sailors.

"What'd you do, tell everyone between mess deck and our berth?"

Carter just smiled. Gossiping like an old lady clearly didn't faze him. With that fresh face of his, it was hard to believe he was a SEAL. Hell, it was hard to believe he was even old enough to serve, let alone two years older than Brody's twenty-nine.

"It was getting interesting, with the recruit mouthing off. And Bad Ass just sitting there counting his winnings. I thought the kid was gonna dive across the table. Then Bad Ass stood up and the wuss realized he was in serious danger of getting his ass handed to him."

"He was a NUB, Farm Boy. He didn't know any better." Brody had been a NUB, or new useless body, once. Fresh out of boot camp and on his first tour, thinking he was ready to take on anything. Anyone.

That kind of thinking had been forcefully adjusted pretty fast.

"Why are you playing with recruits?" Masters asked.

"I'd already cleaned out the officers," Brody admitted with a grin.

"Trouble," Masters muttered again, but he was laughing as he said it.

"We don't reach port till morning. What was I supposed to do? Sit in here like a good boy reading a book?" And the crew was providing Brody with a fat wad of poker winnings.

Masters snickered, then angled the book to one side. "I wasn't reading a book. I'm writing home."

Brody gave a jerk of his shoulder to show it was all the same to him. Truth be told, in his ten years of service he'd read a lot more books than he'd written letters home.

"You settle it or are we gonna be getting company?"

"It's done. He just didn't like losing." Too bad, since Brody liked winning. Not enough to cheat, though. He didn't need to. He was damned good. Something he made a point of being, with anything he cared about. Thankfully, that list was pretty short, so he wasn't spreading himself too thin.

"Mail call."

"You get demoted to mailman?" Brody grinned at Lieutenant Blake Landon. As officers went, the guy was all G.I. As friends went, Blake was aces.

"Nah, I came to make sure you weren't hiding a body."

"Did you have to tell everybody?" Brody gave Carter an exasperated look.

"I heard one of the seamen talking about a hosing some booter got in a poker game and how he was schooled by some visiting badass."

"And used mail delivery as an excuse to come by to make sure I didn't do more than pull rank?" Brody guessed.

"Maybe I just wanted to see your pretty face," Blake shot back, dumping a handful of letters on Brody's cot. "Or find out if you'd lost a bet and had to find yourself some pen pals. You're not known for your communication skills, pal."

"Snipers don't have to do a whole lot of socializing."

"Good thing. 'Cause you suck at it."

True. Probably another reason that Brody almost never got mail. He didn't do relationships. Oh, the occasional weekend fling or a few dates, but no woman had been able to hold his interest longer than a leave lasted. Definitely not long enough to reach the letter-sending stage. Sure, his gramma sent a letter and cookies every month, something that still made him squirm a little. But nobody else wrote. Hell, everyone else he knew was navy. His team here on the ship, or his platoon back in Coronado.

He snatched up the letters, all four of them, and glanced at the package. Yep, cookies from Irene. He tossed her letter on top of the box to read later and thumbed through the others. His brow creased. They all had Bedford return addresses. Two he recognized.

"Letters from home?"

Brody lifted the two while frowning at the third. "Guys I used to run with. I didn't know they could write."

"And that one?" Blake asked, poking his finger toward the last, the one with the flowing feminine writing. "Girlfriend?"

"From Bedford?" Brody's laugh held no humor. "Hardly."

No need to say more than that. Once, on a drunken bender, Brody had shared the details of his first hitch in the navy with Blake. Since the lieutenant had about the same love for his hometown and the people there, he'd gotten it.

Blake, ever the Boy Scout, didn't push the uncomfortable subject. Instead, he thumped his knuckles on the box he'd delivered.

"You bringing the cookies to Friday's poker game?" he asked, referring to their monthly game whenever they were on base in Coronado.

"Without a doubt," Brody confirmed. Irene's snickerdoodles were worth a buck apiece; her macadamia white chocolate anted up for five. And her fudge brownies? Those babies were pure gold.

Blake handed the other guys their much bigger bundles of mail and, after warning Brody to stay out of trouble, left them to enjoy their letters from home.

And Brody to stare at his.

The only woman who'd ever written him was his grandmother.

Not because he avoided women. But letter writing was nowhere on the list of things he did with them. Nope, they were a sweeter treat than the box full of cookies sitting on Brody's pillow. And they lasted about as long, too.

While Masters and Carter ripped through their mail, Brody looked at the envelope again.

Curiosity fought intuition. He wanted to know what woman'd be writing to him. But he had a strong feeling that opening that letter was gonna end up on his already-too-long list of things he regretted.

So he tossed it on his pillow, tearing open the one from Skeet Magee instead. It didn't take long to skim the page. There were only a handful of sentences.

Shit.

He blew out a heavy breath, hoping it'd relieve some of the pressure suddenly pushing on his chest.

He hated death.

Brody stared at the wall, seeing nothing but a gray blur.

He'd served on dozens of missions in his five years as a SEAL. He'd killed, and he'd watched death. He'd lost buddies and he'd mourned. That was the name of the game. A simple fact every soldier, sailor and military personnel faced.

So why was this hitting him so hard?

Knowing who the third letter was from now, filled with even more reluctance than before, he lifted the slender envelope off his pillow. The soft scent of something flowery filled his senses. Whether it was the paper itself or just a memory, he didn't know.

Sorta as though he was in a dream, Brody slid his nail under the flap, careful not to tear the writing. Wetting his lips, he took a breath and pulled out the letter.

Dear Brody,

I know it's been a long time, and I'm sure I'm the last person you want to hear from. But I felt it was important that I write, that I let you know that we've lost Joe. He never quite made it out of that self-destructive cycle, and after you left town, he sank deeper into ugly gang activity. He was in San Quentin on robbery charges and got killed last month in a fight.

*I know the two of you stayed in touch. I found
your letters, a couple of photos, in Joe's things.*
  Please, write me back.

It was like being sucked, unwillingly, into a pit of memories. None good, except the ones that involved tasting
Genna. Brody didn't deny his life before the navy. He
wasn't proud of it, but neither was he ashamed.

But Genna was more than just a specter from his past.

He didn't think about her every day. He didn't dream
about her every night. He wasn't that big of a sap. But he
wasn't a liar either.

He thought of her.

A lot.

Too much.

In the navy, he'd found his calling. He'd found his pride.
He'd found himself.

And in a weird way, he had Genna Reilly to thank for it.

But he couldn't.

It was easier to keep the door to the past closed. To try
not to think about her, or everything that'd led up to his
ignominious entry into the navy. Too much.

And now Joe was dead.

And Genna wanted him to write her back.

Why?

What the hell was there to say?

Why'd they have to kick that door open?

All of a sudden, fury like he hadn't felt in years pounded
through him.

"Genius, got something I can write with?"

Masters spun a pad of paper across the room, Frisbee-
style. Brody caught the pen that followed, glaring at them
both for a second before taking a breath.

He sketched out a short sentence. Then, still riding on
a wave of anger he couldn't explain, he shoved the paper

into an envelope, used Genna's as a reference to address it and licked it closed.

Then, ignoring his cookie ante and the other letters, he headed for the gym to beat the hell out of something. Anything. Sweat, hard work and pushing his physical limits had saved him before. Maybe it would again.

GENNA REILLY HATED DATING. Seriously hated it. She'd almost be willing to marry the next guy who asked just to never have to date again. Almost.

It wasn't the interaction that bothered her—she loved people. And it wasn't that she was anti-relationships. She'd had a few, she'd given them her all. But inevitably they'd left her wondering what was the point. Now, she was just holding out for a great relationship. Her dream relationship. Which didn't include this "good-night at the door" awkwardness that made her want to scream.

"This was great. I'm glad we finally got to go out," Stewart said in a hearty tone, one foot forward already prepared to follow her into the house. For what? Coffee? They'd had it with dessert. A second round of dessert on her couch? Ha. Genna didn't think so.

"Thanks so much for the lovely evening." Before he could lean in for a kiss, Genna offered her brightest smile and slipped through the screen door, keeping her expression cheerful and giving a little finger wave. After a long second and a flash of irritation, he nodded and turned to go. She waited only until he cleared the bottom step before shutting the door.

Leaning against it, she held her breath and listened for the sound of his car. Too many of the guys she dated seemed to choose this point in the evening to suddenly forget their cell phones and need to make a call, or have a bathroom emergency, or worse, think she needed convincing that the night was so awesome it couldn't be over yet.

"Fun time?"

Genna pried her lids open to give her temporary roommate a dead-eyed stare.

"Fun? The guy collects troll dolls, Macy."

The pretty brunette snickered once before plastering a proper look of conciliatory concern on her face. It was hard to hold it with all that newly engaged, soon-to-be-a-bride smugness she was wallowing in, though.

"Troll dolls? Those ugly little things with all the hair? He was probably just joking. C'mon, he's an attorney with great prospects. I don't think you're giving him a chance."

Genna wrinkled her nose. How much of a chance did a girl have to give? Either the guy made her heart go pitty-pat or he didn't. And Stewart definitely didn't. Genna wanted a guy who made her feel special with just a glance. A guy she could count on to be her own true hero. She shouldn't have to work at it.

"I went out with him, didn't I?" She dropped onto the couch next to Macy, who was multitasking her way through addressing her wedding invitations, eating a disgusting-looking diet bar and watching reruns of *Friends*. "I'd have had a better time staying here with you. Lousy food choices and all."

"Quite a statement, considering how much you love your food." Macy winked before taking a bite of the dry-looking carob-coated cardboard she claimed was going to slim her down a dress size in three months. "But one date isn't enough. You need to give guys more of a chance. When's the last time you went out with someone a second time?"

Genna sighed. First dates were testing grounds. Nobody got hurt if she said no after a first date. But second dates built expectations. Made guys think there was a chance.

"If I know on the first date that I'm not interested, why

would I go on a second date? That just leads to hurt feelings."

"That's silly," Macy said dismissively.

"Oh, yeah? I dated Kyle for a year, and when we broke up, he moved away he was so upset. I dated that dentist for two weeks, and when I didn't accept his invitation to a cruise to Greece, my mother cried for a week. My father pouted all through Christmas when I didn't go out with his new deputy after a few dates." Genna threw her hands in the air, as if to say *so there*.

"But that's the point. Those were all perfectly nice guys. I don't understand why you wouldn't go out with them longer."

"Because I didn't feel anything for them," Genna said, the words tight with frustration. Why didn't anyone accept that she didn't want to settle for just any guy? She wanted a special guy.

"But you're in a rough place right now. Maybe the date wasn't that bad, you just didn't want to be there?"

Although delivered in a gentle tone, the words had the blunt force intensity that only two decades of friendship could offer.

"I'm not in a rough place," Genna denied. "I just wasn't interested."

"And your brother was murdered two months ago," Macy reminded her quietly.

Genna wanted to ask what that had to do with her lousy date. But they both knew it had everything to do with it.

Stewart Davis had moved to town a year ago. Being a lawyer, he'd gotten to know her father fairly well—and had quickly become the answer to Sheriff and Mrs. Reilly's prayers. The perfect potential son-in-law.

But Genna had repeatedly turned down his invitations, not interested despite everyone's claims that they'd be perfect for each other. Until two months ago, after Joe's funeral. He'd asked her out in front of her father, and the way her dad's eyes had lit up, she hadn't been able to refuse.

So in addition to disowning his family, causing no end of stress for their parents, stealing her car and putting her in the unwanted position of the favored perfect child, she was laying blame for this date on Joe, too.

Damn him.

She sniffed, wiping a tear off her chin and looking at her fingers blankly. None of those were things to mourn. Why was she crying?

"It'll get better," Macy promised with a sympathetic pat on Genna's knee. "And your next date will be better, too. Maybe give it a week or so. Give yourself time to heal."

"I don't want to go out with Stewart again."

"You should, though." Macy shrugged off Genna's glare. "What? It's only fair. And your dad wants you to, your mom is over the moon at the idea of you dating a lawyer and you need to do whatever you can right now to help them out, to make them happy."

She paused and took another bite of her carob-coated cardboard, then offered a questioning look, as if daring Genna to deny it.

She wished she could. She felt like all she did was try to make her parents happy. The worse Joe behaved, the harder it hit their parents. The more miserable they were, the better she behaved to try to make up for it. It'd been a vicious circle.

Joe's first arrest and time in jail had put their mother in the hospital, making Genna give up her plans for Stanford to stay close to home. Joe's first stint in rehab had been followed by Genna's quitting her job in San Diego because the hour-and-a-half commute worried her father. By the time Joe had hit prison, she was working the most boringly safe job imaginable to go with her boringly safe life. It wasn't as if she wanted to jump out of airplanes or hitchhike across the country. But, man, she wished she had a little excitement in her life.

Instead, she'd been *this close* to being fitted for wings and a halo when Joe had been killed.

Now she didn't know where she stood. If he was done behaving horribly, didn't that mean she could ease up on trying to be perfect? Guilt poured through her, sticky and sour, turning her stomach.

"I'm getting something to eat," Genna said quickly, pushing off the couch as if she could run from her thoughts.

"You have mail on the counter."

Genna muttered her thanks as she headed straight for the freezer. She pulled out a pint of double-fudge ice cream, then got the milk from the fridge. She grabbed the jar of caramel sauce she'd made the previous week for good measure. Hopefully, it'd be hard to be sad while slurping down a chocolate milk shake with extra caramel.

Waiting for the blender to work its magic, she flipped through her mail with about as much interest as she'd felt in that date. Which was just about zip.

Then she came to a letter with an APO postal cancellation. There was no name, nor an address, so there was no way to know who it was from.

But she did.

Hands shaking, Genna didn't even notice dropping the rest of the mail on the counter as she held up the letter in both hands. Heart racing, she wet her lips, wanting to open it. Terrified to see what he'd said.

Ten years ago, Brody Lane had shown her an all-too-brief glimpse of awesome. In return, she'd landed him in the navy. She hadn't known where he'd gone at first. Partly because she'd spent a month on in-house restriction, partly because nobody—not her parents, not anyone in town, nobody—was saying a word. It wasn't until Joe had gotten out of the county lockup that he'd told her what Brody had done, had sacrificed. Because of her.

She stared at the letter, a little ragged and worn-looking against the soft pink of her manicure. She was the one who'd made this reconnection by writing him. She'd always wanted to. Always wished she'd had the nerve to tell him she was sorry for her part in landing him in the navy. But she'd been afraid. Afraid he'd hated her for it.

He was like the bridge between the two sides of her life. That side, fabulous and fun, filled with possibilities and excitement and wild times. And this side, with its day-in-and-day-out practicality, focused on doing what was smart, what was right, being perfect.

And she was scared that opening the envelope would somehow suck her right back to the other side of the bridge.

And even more terrified at how much she wanted to go there.

Figuring it'd be confetti soon the way she was shaking, she grabbed her brass letter opener, and with a deep breath, slit the envelope open. She gently pulled the thin paper out and, without blinking, unfolded it.

And stared.

Frowned and blinked. Then stared harder.

"Is he kidding?" she asked the empty room in bafflement. Then she looked at the paper again.

What are you wearing?

What was she wearing?

That was it?

She'd risked family disapproval, her father's fury, and had sucked up every last bit of nerve she had to write to him. She'd sent horrible news, informing him of the downward spiral and death of a guy who'd once been his best friend.

And this was how he responded?

Grinding her teeth, Genna held the letter out at arm's length, peering at it again. But the words didn't change.

What was she freaking wearing?

Jaw set, more alive than she'd felt in forever, she stormed over to the small rolltop desk in the corner and grabbed her stationery box. She yanked out a sheet of paper, ripping it in the process. She snatched up another and let her pen fly across the page.

She'd show him.

*A teeny, tiny nightie the same shade as your Harley.
You remember the Harley, don't you? Midnight-blue,
so pretty it glowed. I used to dream you'd take me for
a ride on that bike. In my dreams, I always thanked
you by taking you for a ride in return. I could do
that, in this little nightie....*

BRODY READ THE letter for the fifth time, still not believing what it said. She was trying to kill him. That had to be it. Somehow, she knew this time he was floating in a submarine in the middle of the Atlantic Ocean with a crew of men.

He looked at the letter again and nodded. Yeah. She was getting revenge for something. Maybe she was pissed that he'd made her scream with pleasure, then hadn't called the next morning. Girls were weird like that, even when the not-calling excuse was being shanghaied into the navy.

Brody realized he was grinning.

How far could he push her? How far was she willing to go?

He grabbed a piece of paper and pen.

Might as well find out.

"DID THE MAIL COME?" Genna asked as soon as she cleared the front door, her arms filled with grocery bags, her purse and the box of fliers the mayor wanted folded just so for distribution.

"It's on the table." Macy gave her a narrow-eyed look. "You've been awfully interested in the mail lately. Are you expecting something important?"

"Important? Nope, not at all." Genna wet her lips, trying to be subtle as she edged toward the kitchen. "I'm just waiting for the latest *Cosmo*. I heard there are some great book recommendations in there."

"Books. In *Cosmo?*" Macy shook her head and went back to sewing tiny roses on an array of tulle circles. "I can just imagine what kind of stories those are. Naughty, right?"

"Very naughty. Red-hot, in fact, I read one last month called *Fearless*. Very hot," Genna said, spying the APO return and dropping her armload of stuff to grab it up. "And speaking of, I'm going to hop in the shower. Long day."

She might have babbled a couple more things as she hurried for the bathroom, her only guaranteed privacy. She loved having Macy here, but it'd sure be nice when her friend was married and Genna had her house to herself again.

The door locked, she twisted the shower on with one hand while ripping the letter open with the other.

You'd look good in a nightie while I bent you over my Harley. But you'd look even better in nothing.
  What'd you taste like? I wonder.
  What do you think I taste like?
  What would it feel like to find out?

Whew.

Genna caught her reflection in the mirror as she puffed out a breath. Her face was red. Not from embarrassment. Nope, that was the color of sexual need. Hot, vivid, intense.

Seeing no other option, she stripped naked, turned off the hot water and slid under the icy spray.

And imagined Brody as she searched for relief.

I'm craving ice cream. Something cold, rich, delicious. I'll share it with you. But you have to eat it off my body. You can choose where to start. But to help you along, I'll pour a little drizzle of caramel sauce here, just below my belly button. Want to lick it up?

BRODY GROANED—actually groaned aloud—reading those words.

He'd always been more of a chocolate than caramel kind of guy, but now he wanted it like nobody's business.

He wanted Genna even more.

Grateful to be back in Coronado, in the relative privacy of the barracks instead of on a ship with a bunch of guys, he closed his eyes and visualized Genna as she'd been the last time he'd seen her. Then he imagined himself pouring caramel sauce over her body. Top down? Bottom up?

Aching hard, his body demanded the only solution possible. One he'd have to provide for himself, since no woman other than Genna would do.

He'd start in the middle.

I'd prefer a Popsicle to ice cream. Something long and hard I could watch you eat. You should run it over your lips first, so they are nice and wet and sweet when I kiss you. Then you can trace it around your nipples. The cold will make them rock-hard, like they're begging me to warm them. I'll do that while you move the Popsicle down to your thighs, leaving a sticky sweet trail for my lips to follow.

I think you're going to need another Popsicle. We melted that one.

GENNA LAY IN HER BED, the dim glow from her bedside light pooling over the blankets, shining on the paper. She imagined Brody, looking like he had ten years ago, writing those words. Pictured his eyes glowing with a wicked light as he watched her pleasure herself. As he brought her pleasure with just his words and the look on his face.

Her fingers slipped under the hem of her nightie, trailing over her skin in the same path he'd suggested she trail the icy treat. Reading the words again, she edged her panties aside and let her fingers go to work.

Nothing cold here.

I hope you like cherry. Because that's the only flavor Popsicles I like.

I'm all sticky now. I need a shower. You can watch, but you can't join me yet. I've turned the water up so hot, the room is filling with steam. The shower nozzle is set to pulse. Fast, hard bursts against my skin, water droplets sliding down my aching flesh. I want you still. But you're not allowed in the shower. So while you watch, I'm going to pleasure myself and pretend it's you. I'll take the showerhead off its hook and slide it down my body. The water pools between my breasts, gurgling and bubbling before pouring down my body. I'm wet. And not just from the shower.

What would you like to do about it?

BRODY DIDN'T KNOW whether to damn Genna Reilly, or worship her. She'd got him into hot water when she was a teenager, now she had him living under a cold shower.

Brody ran a towel over his head, the rough terry soaking up the droplets and quickly drying his short hair.

Just the thought of a shower brought to mind Genna's last letter.

Of course, so did taking a shower. Seeing water. Hell, just breathing had the words flashing through his brain.

Scowling, Brody threw the towel on his bunk and grabbed his fatigues, shoving one foot in, then the other with enough force he was surprised the fabric didn't rip.

He wasn't writing her back.

This whole crazy game had to stop.

If he didn't respond, neither would Genna.

And they could both get back to living their lives.

He didn't fool himself into thinking he'd forget about the letters over time. If he closed his eyes, he could still remember the taste of her that night in the garage. He could still hear her soft cries of pleasure and see the rosy flush on her skin. Ten years hadn't dimmed that memory.

So, no. The images weren't going anywhere.

But the game was.

Brody finished dressing on autopilot, his brain ricocheting between the plan for the coming mission and every contingency. Their strategy was solid, they'd be solid.

"Lane. Heads up. The helo is ready to fly."

Brody nodded. All suited up now, so was he.

Time to rock and roll.

Habit had him glancing around before shutting the locker, making sure he'd left no traces of anything personal. Nothing was left out except the letter. Brody grabbed it, ready to tuck it away with his few personal effects. But it was like Genna's loopy handwriting was curled around his fingers, not letting go.

Damn. Brody felt like a fool.

He looked to the left, then to the right to make sure he was alone. He grimaced at his behavior, then pulled the letter from the envelope to read it one more time.

4

TIME TO ROCK AND ROLL. Brody, along with the rest of the team, loaded onto the Chinook helicopter. They didn't have to go over the mission. It was etched in their minds, every aspect of it not only committed to memory, but muscle memory. They were machines, ready to engage.

He eyed the extra guy in the bird, separate from the team. Watching. He didn't acknowledge them and as far as the team was concerned, he was just cargo.

Government cargo.

All SEAL missions were covert. Top secret was the name of the game, whether it was a direct action, recon or rescue.

Which usually meant no audience.

He puffed out a gust of air, then strapped himself in as the bird started liftoff. This wasn't his first rescue mission by far. But he figured it would be the first time he'd ever have the opportunity to meet the Cin C's right hand. He looked toward the passenger one more time, then dismissed him.

Tee minus five.

While the blades of the helo whirled their deafening hum, everybody went into prep mode.

The usual banter flew through the team as they did one last equipment check.

And then they went silent.

Brody had never worried about clearing his head before a mission. In the ten years he'd served in the navy, he'd learned a few things. Focus. Discipline. And confidence. Not the cocky bravado he'd perfected as a teen. But the absolute assurance that he was damned good at what he did and didn't have a thing to prove to anyone.

He was a finely honed weapon, trained with the necessary skills to carry out this rescue mission. He didn't have a single doubt that he'd do his job, and do it well. Because he had nothing, nobody, in the world that meant a damned thing to him except his team. His platoon. His duty.

He glanced around the belly of the plane. Cormack had his head tilted back, eyes closed as he muttered Buddhist chants. Masters looked fierce, as if he was going over the plan one more time in his head. But Brody knew he wasn't. The plan was imprinted; they didn't need to review it. Nope, the guy was mentally reciting *The Iliad.*

Brody usually thought about nothing at this point.

This time, just before he flipped the switch and became a military machine, the image of Genna Reilly filled his head. Her smile warming his belly, the wicked delight in her eyes reminding him of his past.

Was she still as bright as the sun, drawing people to her like a spotlight? Did her laugh gurgle the way it had when she was younger, deep and husky? And just how would she look in that little blue nightie she kept writing to him about? Or more to the point, how would she look out of it?

Was she still as sexy? Her hair a heavy curtain of long black silk, like in his fantasies? Did she make those same noises when she came? Or was sex just a way to pass time for her now? Like it was for him.

It was her smile that became his focal point as he let all

thoughts fall away. He shifted his shoulders, shrugging off everything but the mission.

"It's time," Landon said. His words were low and calm. His expression contained. He scanned the team, gave a nod. "Let's kick ass."

GENNA WAS GOING crazy with boredom.

It was like there was a switch in her head that enabled her to get through the same old boring job, blah life, day in-and-day-out monotonous yawn-fest of good behavior. And that switch had flipped off.

She knew she should find a way to flip it back on.

But she didn't want to.

If she did, she'd have to go back to making other people happy. Which still included Mr. Perfect, the troll collector, and all the pressures to go out with him on a second date.

The guy was boring.

Especially when compared with other people who needed to remain nameless, even in her own mind. People who wrote letters that made her melt before she'd even opened the envelope. People who were out living their lives, making a difference. People who, even though they didn't even sign their name to their letters, made her want so much.

Wish that things had turned out differently.

Lunchtime chatter faded into a buzz as Genna contemplated what her life might be like if she'd never taken that dare ten years ago. Or better yet, if her father hadn't ruined the best night of her life. If she'd rebelled instead of trying to soothe her miserable parents, and had done all the things she'd hoped to.

While her friends ordered dessert, she looked around with a sigh. She was like this café. Nice enough, but nothing exciting. Kinda like Millie, the café owner who kept the menu exactly the same month after month, year after year, so as not to upset her regulars by shaking things up.

"So that's an apple crisp with ice cream and a fruit bowl," the plump waitress ticked off, pointing her pencil at each woman as she recited their order. When her pencil aimed at Genna, she asked, "How about you? You want the last scoop of crisp? Or maybe some pie?"

With the nearest bakery in the next town, places like Millie's Café did their own baking. Genna eyed the display case. The toasted, almost-black meringue on the lemon pie was sliding to one side like a drunken mushroom cap.

"I'll pass." She softened her refusal with a smile. She'd stop by her house on the way back to the office and grab a couple of the turtle brownies she'd made yesterday instead. Maybe she'd take the rest of the tray back to the mayor's office. Last time she'd brought in treats for the city council meeting, everyone had raved. As they had when she'd baked for the school fundraiser, and her mom's ladies' tea. Sometimes Genna felt as if baking were the only area of her life where she was allowed to be free. Creative. To explore and experiment and indulge.

"Genna!"

"What?" Blinking a couple of times, Genna forced her attention back to her lunch companions. Macy was making notes in her wedding planner, but Dina was glaring.

"You aren't listening."

"Of course I am. You were saying you had juicy news."

"I do. And it's the juiciest. Better than anything you've got."

Dina figured her job at the hairdresser's should guarantee her the best gossip access, so it tended to drive her crazy that Genna often got better dirt first.

"Is it the news from this morning?" Genna asked.

"What news?"

"That Maury McCaskle ran the red light on Beeker

Street because he was yelling at his wife on the cell phone again?"

"Even bigger."

"That he was yelling at her because he found out about her affair with the pizza-delivery boy?"

"Bigger than that."

Genna's eyes rounded in faux shock. "Bigger? The pizza boy is only sixteen. How can you out-gossip that?"

This was what her life had come to, Genna realized with a morose sigh. Gossiping with her friends over a long lunch was the baddest she got to be. She thought of her little pen-pal project and her sigh turned dreamy. Now that was bad. So, so deliciously bad.

As bad as only a bad boy knew how to be.

Images filled her head, so vivid she swore she could reach out and touch them. Taste them. Feel them.

Thankfully, their waitress chose that moment to return with their order.

Whew, baby, it was much too hot in here for February. Even for sunny Southern California. Genna gratefully gulped down half the iced caffeine.

"This isn't gossip. It's more like news. Big, juicy exciting news," Dina said as she dug into her dessert.

Genna grimaced at the sight of the soft, cream-colored crisp. What'd they done? Scooped the leftover oatmeal from breakfast over canned apple pie filling and popped it in the toaster oven? At least they'd drizzled caramel over the vanilla ice cream.

"You just like to say it's news because gossip sounds so ugly," Macy said dismissively.

Easily ignoring them, Genna contemplated the many uses for caramel sauce. She'd offered up the sweet treat as a naughty suggestion in one of her letters to Brody. Especially her homemade caramel. Sticky sweet and buttery rich. She'd warm it up first, then drizzle it over her body and invite Brody to lick it up. She'd even let him choose. He could start at her toes and nibble his way up or start at her shoulders and taste his way down.

"When my information has to do with Brody Lane, I'd say it's news," Dina snapped.

Genna gave a start, almost spilling her tea. How had Dina peeked into her mind and pulled Brody's name out? What else had she seen while she was there?

"Brody?" she breathed. Excitement and fear hit her in equal doses, along with a big wave of lust.

"I was doing Irene Lane's hair this morning. She's Brody's gramma, you know." Dina waited for them all to nod, as if she'd just revealed some juicy tidbit. Since Genna spent every Saturday afternoon with Irene, she was pretty solid on who the woman was. "Do you remember when he ran away? What was he, thirteen? I heard he lived on the streets in L.A., a part of one of the uglier gangs and getting into all kinds of trouble. Four years he was running wild on his own until he was shot in the chest before his dad hauled him home."

He was fourteen, gone three years and knifed in the belly before his gramma had brought him home after he'd gotten out of the hospital. But Genna didn't correct Dina as she usually would. Talking about Brody made her nervous.

"I only have a half hour left of my lunch break," Macy interjected, her expression impatient. "Get to the point or get out of my way so I can refill my drink."

Dina sniffed, but didn't move out of the booth. Instead she leaned in toward the center of the table and with her most gleeful expression, whispered, "Brody Lane is coming back to town."

Genna choked on her tea.

"What? No way."

Brody, back here? Where she could see him? Touch

him? Hear his voice as he said all those words he'd put to paper?

Holy hell, she was in trouble.

"Brody Lane, back in town?" exclaimed their waitress, hurrying over as if proximity would get her more information.

"Yep, he's coming back in a couple of weeks. Irene said he was injured. Really bad. He was doing something military. He's army or a marine or something like that."

"He's navy," Genna corrected automatically. "He's a navy SEAL."

When three pairs of eyes locked on her, she gave an irritated shrug.

"What, he kept in touch with Joe. They were friends, remember. It's not like I'm in contact with the guy or anything," Genna lied. Not waiting for their response, she gave Dina a ferocious frown. "What happened? How was he injured? How bad is it?"

"And why is he coming here?" Macy added, sounding as though Dina had just announced the coming of Satan and his dancing minions.

"I don't know. All Irene would say was that she wanted her hair set extra tight so it'd hold during her flight to visit Brody in the hospital. She said he'd been hurt in a big mission. That they're calling him a hero now. After she left, I went on the internet. But I couldn't find a single bit of news. They are so weird about hiding all that military stuff. Like it's some big secret or something."

"Right. Military strategy and national security are such silly reasons to make it harder to share good gossip," Genna declared with an exaggerated eye roll. "I don't see why they don't post mission details and the names of all the Special Forces personnel on a website."

The brunette huffed, giving Genna an irritated look.

"Why are they calling Brody Lane a hero?" Genna

asked, figuring an opening to finish her story would pull her out of her snit. "Does that have something to do with how he got hurt and why he's hospitalized?"

"It does," Dina breathed, just as gleeful at sharing the gossip as she was with the attention. "I couldn't get much out of Irene. Just that Brody was on a rescue mission. It must have been someone really important, too. But something happened and Brody was hurt. Another guy even died. What do you think they were doing? I mean, Irene didn't even say where it'd happened."

Dina stopped to take a breath and preen a little because everybody in the room was hanging on her words. Even the waitresses had stopped pretending they weren't listening. Speculation flew, everything from the last big news story to involve the navy SEALs to people mulling names of navy personnel they might contact to get more inside dirt.

Genna didn't pay much attention, though. She was too busy trying to quell the miserable nausea churning in her belly at the realization that Brody could have died.

If it wasn't for her, he wouldn't be in the navy. Wouldn't be putting his life on the line for his country. His sweet, terrified-to-travel gramma wouldn't be getting her hair curled uncomfortably tight.

How badly was he hurt? Was he going to live? Would he be able to keep serving in the navy? Or was the injury so bad he'd be crippled? She imagined him lying in some sterile hospital bed, forever broken.

She pressed her lips together, breathing through her nose and trying to focus on something else. Anything else.

Brody healthy and whole. Strong and silent.

Or not so silent when it came to writing.

Letting the words he'd sent her fill her mind, she focused on them until her stomach settled.

Genna stared at the pastry crumble and soggy apples on Dina's plate as if they were about to sprout wings and fly. Brody Lane. Hot. Oh, yeah. Her blood heated and her mouth went dry. Brody, of the broad shoulders, tight ass and clever way with words. Who knew a guy who barely linked twelve words together at a time could turn her on with just the stroke of his, um, pen?

"If he's hurt, how's he coming back here?" Macy asked, interrupting Genna's hot little mental journey. "You said Irene is flying out there. Where is there?"

"He's in a military hospital in Virginia. She said she's gonna convince him to come back here as soon as they release him. How she thinks that's gonna happen is beyond me, though. Nobody has ever convinced Brody Lane to do anything he didn't want to."

"Here? Why here?" Macy said, her fingers pressed to her lips. "Shouldn't he recover in a hospital or tent or something?"

"You're so mean," Dina chided Macy. "Even the president of the United States thinks this guy is a hero, Macy. He might have been a little trouble when he was a teenager, but who wasn't? He's been serving his country for ten years. You'd think you could get over judging him by now."

It was all Genna could do not to roll her eyes. Every one of Dina's words had been playing to their audience, her way of looking righteous and caring.

Still, the recital had its intended effect. Macy blinked fast, her cheeks pink as everyone frowned. And from the looks on people's faces, Genna knew word that Brody Lane was a hero was going to be the gossip highlight of the week.

"What'd you mean about the president?" Genna asked quietly, glad that Brody would finally be talked about with respect. Even if it was only in gossipy whispers.

"Oh, did I forget to mention that?" Dina paused, pretending she wasn't aware that the entire room was holding their breath to hear the rest of her announcement. "The president of the U.S. of A. showed up at the hospital where Brody's at and pinned him with a Purple Heart. That's, like, rare according to Irene. She said he offered his personal thanks, and shook Brody's hand."

The room exploded as whispers turned to gasps, excited titters to loud exclamations. The president and Brody Lane? Fingers were flying over cell phones, and the few old-timers who didn't text were calling for their bill.

So much for the gossip being made in whispers.

Genna started to sigh at the ridiculousness of it all, then she caught her breath. Excitement sparked, still having everything to do with Brody, but this time having nothing to do with the image of him naked.

Maybe she could help fan the flames, bring this news to the attention of the right people. People who could make sure Brody got his due. People her father couldn't intimidate just because he was holding a grudge.

Finally, Bedford would see Brody as a hero. The same hero she'd always thought him to be.

She couldn't change the past. But maybe this would make up for it a little. And wouldn't it be fabulous if everyone thinking he was totally awesome helped her father see how great Brody was? That way, if anything did happen between her and Brody, he wouldn't have such a lousy reaction this time.

She almost laughed aloud at the perfection of her plan.

Not that she was thinking anything was going to happen between her and Brody. Not really. Although those letters could be taken as interest on his part. Or severe horniness, she warned herself, not wanting to get her hopes up too high. It wasn't like he'd even used her name. He could have been writing to anyone. But he'd sent the letters to her. That might mean something.

She propped her chin on her fist and gave a wistful sigh. Maybe.

"Do you guys remember that night we played truth or dare and Brody was the—"

"Did Irene say when she'll be back with Brody?" Genna interrupted Dina, looking up so fast she slapped herself in the eyes with her own hair. No, no, no. They were not revisiting truth-or-dare night. She'd never told them what'd happened between her and Brody. She'd played it off as if her father had busted them before anything had happened.

Nobody had ever connected that night and Brody's disappearance, either. Brian Lane had never said a word about his son's departure and if Irene knew Genna's part in her grandson's sudden desire to serve his country, she'd never let on.

Dina blinked a couple of times, clearly not happy to have her juicy gossip flow interrupted. Then, as if she'd just remembered that their little dare was a secret, and one that Genna had paid dearly for with a monthlong restriction, she made a show of dropping the subject.

"Subtle," Macy murmured, rolling her eyes.

Dina huffed. Then, realizing nobody else was paying them any attention, she shrugged and dug into her dessert.

"Irene said he's due to be released from the hospital next week. So depending on how long it takes to convince him, anytime between then and never."

Genna pressed her lips together and stared at the bland blob of dessert Dina was shoveling in, trying to keep her excitement to herself.

A week.

She might see Brody Lane again in a week.

It was going to be so awesome.

WELL, WASN'T THIS freaking awesome.

One minute his life was rolling along just fine.

The next it totally sucked.

He'd come full circle. Ten years ago he'd been a loser

badass with no prospects and a chip on his shoulder. He'd ridden to the top, an elite Special Forces SEAL living a life he loved. And now he was back in his hometown with no prospects, sporting that same chip. He figured it'd take about three days in Bedford before he could claim the loser title again.

His hands fisted around his crutches, Brody glared at the small house, its chipped paint and shutters sagging as if it was as enthusiastic to see him as he was it.

"Brody, sweetie, you sure you want to stay out here? I've got plenty of room in the front house. You can stay with me, where I can do a little fussing over you."

He wanted to be left alone. He wanted to be as far from fussing and people and, hell, life if he had his way.

But he couldn't yell that at his gramma.

Not because manners forbade it or that it was bad form. But because when he'd tried it in the hospital she'd smacked him upside the head, then burst into tears. He hadn't even felt the smack, but the tears had kicked his ass.

He'd given in to the guilt, and the nagging, and when the doctor ordered him to physical therapy at his home base in Coronado, he'd said he'd stay off-base with his family and come in for PT.

He hadn't wanted to return. He didn't want to face his team, to stay on base and pretend he belonged there. That he was still a SEAL.

His leg was jacked up bad. Shrapnel did a nasty number on flesh and muscle. But it'd heal. Unlike Carter.

Dead didn't heal.

The mission had been deemed a success by their superiors, as they'd achieved their target and rescued not only their target but three other hostages.

The mission has been a failure in the eyes of the team. Because they'd lost one of their own.

The mission had been the end as far as Brody was concerned. The warriors' creed demanded they leave no man behind. Dead or alive, they brought out their own.

He'd failed. It didn't matter that he'd taken a hit; he was trained to ignore injuries. It didn't matter that he'd had a little girl in his arms at the time of the explosion that'd knocked Carter on his ass. The only thing that mattered was he hadn't gone back. He hadn't gotten his teammate out in time.

Forcing aside the churning emotions battling it out in his gut, Brody turned to give his gramma a smile. Well, a shift of his lips. That was about as close as he was getting.

"I'll be fine here. I'm better on my own for a while."

For a while. Forever. Either worked for him.

"Now that you're out of the navy—"

"I'm not out," he snapped. Then, grinding his teeth to try to chew the rough edges off his tone, he continued, "I'm on convalescent leave."

Three freaking months of leave before a navy surgeon would reevaluate Brody's chances of full use of his leg. Twelve weeks to contemplate the end of the career he loved.

Once again, Bedford was akin to purgatory just before he dove into hell. He'd vowed when he left—or was kicked out, to be precise—never to set foot in this lousy town again. So why was he back?

He looked at his gramma and sighed. Why? Guilt. That's why. When an old woman who was terrified to fly crossed the country to pray at your bedside, you did whatever the hell she wanted.

Guilt, and the simple truth. He had nowhere else to go.

"Don't you think you'll convalesce better in the main house? There's a phone there, television. I can cook for you and make sure you're okay. These steps, they're not good for your leg. Or for my arthritis. Wouldn't you rather be close where I can keep an eye on you?"

Brody's ears sank into his shoulders.

How many times in his life had Gramma Irene tried to keep an eye on him? So many. Living with his father meant a filthy apartment over a bar, fending for himself from the time he was six onward. As Brian's drinking got worse, it'd included beatings that had escalated until Brody was old enough to hold his own. But it'd also meant freedom.

Gramma Irene's meant rules. Three meals, on time with clean hands. Curfew, attending school and talking. Oh God, the talking.

About his day. His dreams. His emotions.

Brody shuddered.

Nope. Guilt only got him to Bedford.

"The guest house is fine." He'd prefer a dark cave in the middle of nowhere. But he'd settle for no cable or phone in a doily-covered dollhouse with flowers on the walls.

"You're a good boy, Brody," she said, reaching up to pat his shoulder with a fragile hand before handing him the key to the guesthouse. "You might not like it. You might not agree with it. But you need this time. You'll heal here. And you'll be able to make some decisions."

He glanced down at the woman next to him, her silver-streaked black hair curled softly around a face lined by more worries than anyone should deal with in a lifetime. When he'd been a teen, Gramma Irene had barely come to his shoulder, she was so tiny. Now she seemed to hit just above his elbow. He'd filled out plenty in the last ten years. A daily regimen of kicking ass did that to a guy. But he hadn't gotten any taller, which meant she'd shrunk.

"There's nothing for me to decide," he told her as he unlocked the door and pushed it open. His face set, he gripped the crutches and navigated the concrete steps, numb to the pain in his leg. Numb to everything.

As far as he was concerned, his life was done. And he didn't give a single damn about what happened next.

5

O~H~, ~MAN~, ~THIS WAS IT~.

Genna stared at Irene's front door, the fresh white paint a glossy contrast against the peeling gray siding.

This was crazy. All she had to do was reach out and knock.

She visited here every week. Came calling with baked goods, cookies or cakes or whatever Irene was hungry for. At first, it'd just been to be nice to a lonely neighbor. But over the last few years, she and the older woman had grown close.

But she wasn't here to see Irene.

A plate of cookies in one hand, she pressed the other against her stomach, where it felt like butterflies were morphing into dragons.

After he'd heard that Brody was to be in town, the mayor wanted to hold a special parade and maybe a benefit luncheon. As community relations liaison it was Genna's job to arrange it. That's why she was here. Not because she was nosy. Or horny.

Well, she was both, but that wasn't why she was here.

She wet her lips, careful not to smudge her lipstick, then wiped her damp palm on her jeans before shifting the plate to it and drying the other. Maybe she should have worn a skirt. Something fancier. She was representing the city, after all.

Maybe she should go home and change. She glanced at her watch. It was close to dinnertime. Maybe she should come back another day. Yeah. Tomorrow. Or next week. That'd give Irene time to visit with her grandson. It was good manners to wait.

Her stomach stopped pitching and a little of the tension seeped from her shoulders at the decision. Which only proved it was the right choice.

With a relieved smile, she started mentally preparing her excuse to offer the mayor and turned toward the steps to leave.

"Genna?"

With a squeak worthy of a cartoon character, Genna jumped. She spun around so fast she damn near landed on her denim-covered butt, almost sending the plate in her hands flying across the tidy porch. Her heart pounded, blood rushing though her head so fast it sounded like a freight train passing by.

It took her three deep breaths before she could respond.

"Hi." She cleared her throat, then tried again. "Hi, Irene. How are you?"

"I'm good, dear. I've been so flustered this week. Flying in planes, it's not good for a body. Isn't today Tuesday? Or did we change our visit and I forgot? I was on my way to a book club meeting, but I can skip that. I'd much rather chat with you."

Looking as if those flights had definitely taken a toll, Irene pulled open the screen door. Genna hesitated. She was officially still on the clock, and supposed to be following her boss's orders. But Irene appeared tired. The lines in her face seemed deeper, dark circles etched under her usually calm eyes.

"I didn't mean to interrupt your plans. I wanted to drop off these cookies. They're a new recipe I made up, and was hoping for feedback," she prevaricated, holding up the plate as proof.

This would work out great. She'd get the inside scoop on Brody before she had to see him. Maybe she could even drop a few hints, mention the parade the mayor wanted to hold in Brody's honor, and get Irene behind the idea.

"Well, this is a treat." Irene stepped back, welcoming Genna into the house. The inside was as cozy and comfortable as the outside run-down, reminding Genna again to research how to scrape siding and look into exterior paint.

"Sit, sit. I'll put on coffee," Irene said, gesturing to the wingback chairs in front of the bay window. Knowing better than to offer to help, Genna sat. Acting as if all her attention was on meticulously pulling the plastic wrap from the lime-green plate, she surreptitiously looked around for signs of Brody.

Like luggage or a jacket.

Or his body.

Nothing.

"Flustered," Irene muttered five minutes later when she returned with the coffee. "I almost forgot your sugar. As if I don't know how you take your coffee. But a couple of days serving it black and I'm all mixed up."

Genna leaned forward to take the cup, murmuring her thanks. Anticipation rushed so fast through her system it was making her jittery. Figuring it was only polite, she waited for the older woman to get comfortable before grilling her about her grandson.

Before she could, though, Irene launched into the woes of traveling. She followed it up with the horrors of airplanes, with a few comments for the kindness of strangers, or the lack thereof.

Genna decided she should have been rude.

They were on their second cup of coffee and third double-fudge cookie and Irene was still talking about those lousy flights.

Yeah, yeah, traveling sucked. Recycled air was the work of the devil and the cost of a tiny drink was akin to highway robbery. She didn't care about the trip, though. She wanted to know about the treat Irene had brought home with her.

"How is Brody doing?" she finally asked, unable to continue politely waiting for the older woman to bring him up first.

Irene frowned. It only took Genna a second to realize it was worry, not annoyance over Genna's interruption.

"He's hurting," Irene finally said, staring into her cup and blinking a few times, as if shooing away tears. "Not just his body. He had horrible internal injuries, two surgeries and they're still not sure if his leg will ever be as strong as it was before. When I walked into that hospital room, I thought they'd lied to me. I thought I'd flown all the way across the country to claim his body, he was so bruised and cut-up and broken-looking."

Genna reached across the small table to curl her hand over Irene's fragile wrist, giving it a gentle rub.

"But he's okay, isn't he?" Oh, please, let him be okay. She'd had nothing to go on but gossip. Those in the know claimed that Brody had arrived with his gramma in a big blue car, and that while he was on crutches, he'd been sporting all his parts. "The surgeries were a success."

"He's alive." Irene pressed her lips together, her face closing up in a look Genna remembered seeing on her grandson's face. In all the years they'd visited, Irene never talked about family business. She might mention Brody in passing, but never did she complain or even brag. Whether it was an inherent dislike of gossip, or a defense against the years of fodder her family had provided, Genna didn't know.

But this time, Irene looked up with tears in those pale brown eyes, two shades darker than her grandson's.

"His body is healing, but more than that was hurt."

"What happened? Are you allowed to say?" Genna had only outright asked about Brody once, and that'd taken every bit of her nerve. Irene had said SEAL business was top secret and that she was doing her part to support her grandson by keeping her mouth shut. Given that Genna's question had been along the lines of *had she heard from him lately,* she'd taken the hint.

"He was on a mission. Something went wrong." Irene shrugged, the movement as helpless as her expression. "He doesn't say anything about it. But I can see the hurt in his eyes."

Her heart weighing heavy in her chest, worry pressing down so hard Genna wanted to cry, she could only shake her head.

"He's going to be okay. He's tough, Irene. He's a SEAL." From everything she'd read, which was everything she could find on SEALs—just out of curiosity—they were the elite, the best of the best.

"I hope so." Irene gave a shaky sigh, then her expression lightened a little and she peered at Genna. "You and Brody were friends when he lived here, weren't you? You're close to the same age, at least."

Her and Brody? Friends?

If she didn't wish that were true so much, Genna would have laughed. Brody as a teen had been gorgeous, sexy and fascinating. And that was from afar. Then she'd discovered his sense of humor and clever mind, to say nothing of his wickedly talented hands and delicious mouth.

And, of course, his writing skills.

But she was pretty sure none of that added up to them

being friends. She frowned. It hardly made them acquaintances.

"He and Joe were friends," Genna said, sidestepping the issue. She didn't talk about that night ten years ago, ever. To this day, she didn't know if Brody's decision to join the navy was his own, or if it'd been forced on him. Her father refused to discuss it, and by the time she was off restriction, Brody was long gone.

"Will you talk to him, Genna? Please, for me?" Irene pleaded, the worry in her eyes adding years to her creased face. "He's been here three days now and said maybe twice that many words."

"Irene—"

"I'm so worried."

Genna started to say she didn't think he wanted to talk to her, then stopped and sighed. For a million reasons, she wanted to talk to Brody. Heck, she was here specifically to do just that. And she wanted to do whatever she could to relieve the worry on her friend's face.

Why bother coming up with excuses she didn't mean?

"I'll talk to him. Is he going to be back soon? Or is he staying at the hotel?" She'd figured if he was, someone would have mentioned it. But he was a SEAL and had all that top secret mojo going for him.

"He's in the guesthouse. Just go on back."

On back? To the tiny building behind the house that faced her own backyard? Genna had thought that was a storage building.

"Now?" Genna was so nervous, the word took on three syllables and ended on a squeak.

"If you don't mind. You can take him some cookies. He does love your cookies," Irene said with a glint in her eyes.

Mind? Of course she didn't mind. Just as soon as she tamed the dragons suddenly doing somersaults in her belly. It was a toss-up what made her more nervous. That she was about to see Brody, for sure. Or that he was spending the next little while sleeping so close to her bedroom.

And Irene didn't give her time to figure it out.

The sweet old lady moved impressively fast, bundling the cookies and Genna out the back door, then standing there to make sure Genna didn't bolt across the alley.

Her fingers were damp again and her knees just a little wobbly. Genna was pretty sure they'd carry her home, though. She glanced over her shoulder and grimaced. Making an eighty-year-old woman run after her was rude, and the look on Irene's face left no room for doubt. Genna had been told to do something, she'd damned well better do it.

She took a deep breath that did nothing but spur the tummy-tumbling dragons to spin faster, and stepped up to the door. Holding the plate so tight her knuckles were white, she lifted the other hand to knock.

Okay, so maybe it was a tap, not a knock. But still…

This was it.

A chance she'd been dreaming about off and on for over ten years. A lot more on than off since she and Brody had started exchanging letters.

She didn't know what she felt.

Excitement, definitely. Brody Lane was her fantasy guy. He inspired feelings, reactions, emotions that she had no business thinking. At least, not while his gramma was watching.

She looked over her shoulder again to check.

Yep. Gramma was watching.

She tried to think nice thoughts instead. Good girl thoughts. Like dating. That was a possibility, right?

It wasn't as if he was off-limits anymore, either.

He was a hero.

The mayor wanted to throw him a parade.

Even her parents couldn't object to her dating a military hero, could they?

Not that she was counting on Brody's wanting to date her. Sexy letters aside, it wasn't as if they knew each other. Not really. And then there was the fact that their one and only kiss had gotten him corralled into the navy.

But who knew. Maybe all that postal flirting was going to turn into something else. There, Genna decided. Nice, delusional thoughts. Totally appropriate to entertain in front of his gramma.

Inspired, she knocked again. This time with enough force to actually make noise.

There was a loud thump inside, then the scraping sound of wood against wood.

Her stomach tumbled over itself.

She stood straighter, pulled back her shoulders and took a deep breath. The move had never done a thing to make her breasts look bigger, but a girl could hope.

The door opened.

Oh, please, let the whimpering sigh be in her head and not aloud.

Oh, my.

The years had been kind, indeed, to Brody Lane.

Even as his expression folded into a scowl when he realized she wasn't who he'd expected to see at his door, she couldn't stop staring.

It was as if Mother Nature had looked at the perfection that had been him at nineteen and decided to add a few layers of "oh, baby" gorgeousness to her work of art.

Arresting before with its sharp planes and brooding features, his face was more intense now. Even sharper, despite being unshaven and shadowed. His eyes were just as striking, like molten gold. They'd always been distant, except when he'd smiled. But now there was a chasm there, as though he was watching from miles away. Assessing. Her, the situation, their past, present and future, all without blinking.

It was kinda scary. Not sure what he was seeing, or more important, what he thought about what he was seeing, Genna bit her lip.

It was nerves as much as curiosity that made her peel her gaze from his to check out his body. And what a body it was.

Broad and muscular, his chest and shoulders looked as though they were sculpted from marble under his black tee. He still had that lean build, his waist tapering to slender hips.

Her eyes dropped lower and she gulped.

Oh, my, the blue cotton sweatpants did nothing to hide the muscle between his legs, either.

Little dots danced in front of her eyes. She realized she'd forgotten to breath.

A gulp of air cleared the dizziness, but the tingling didn't go away.

He was… Wow.

The things he could do with that body, she'd bet they were nothing short of amazing. And she wasn't just talking military things. Her mouth was dry and she was starting to feel a little dizzy again.

So she forced her gaze to climb back up to his face.

His unwelcoming scowl had turned into a ferocious frown.

She wrinkled her nose. She should have kept checking out the bod. He obviously wasn't thrilled to have company.

So what else was new?

"Hi, Brody. I brought you some cookies." As greetings went, it was lame. But she added her best smile. When that had no reaction, she held up the plate as proof. And, yes, as a bribe.

He didn't even look at the plate. Her lips threatened to drop into a pout.

"Um, it's me. Genna." She paused, brows arched. She

tried a friendly smile that was only a little shaky with nerves. When he didn't even blink, she swallowed hard, then added, "Joe's sister."

Your favorite pen pal, she wanted to say. But given his reaction so far, she was a little afraid to bring that up.

Genna waited. After five seconds, her smile dimmed. At thirty, she was straight-up frowning. Knowing a glare was imminent at sixty, she crossed her arms over her chest, the cookie plate hitting her in the shoulder, and lifted her chin.

"Well? Aren't you even going to say hello?"

Now her scowl matched his.

So much for dating. She couldn't even get the guy to talk to her.

BRODY KNEW THERE were many levels of hell. Why Genna Reilly had to keep showing up on his was surely a way of punishing him for any of his hundreds of infractions.

Did she have to look so damned good while she did it, though?

Why hadn't she aged in ten years?

She should have packed on some weight. Gotten bad skin. Hell, even a lousy haircut would be something.

But, no...

There she stood, long and leggy, her body still as slender as a dream. Her curves were more a whisper than a shout. Nature's way of keeping the attention on her gorgeous face, he figured. Her hair was shorter than she'd worn it as a teen, hitting her shoulders instead of flowing down her back. And those huge eyes, with their exotic tilt and lush lashes, were narrowed with irritation.

He didn't care.

He hadn't invited her here, so why should he play gracious host?

"Are you going to say anything?" she asked, sounding

exasperated. "Hello would be nice. Or even hi if you're only up for a single syllable. I'll settle for a grunt. Or if that's too much, you can simply step out of the doorway and gesture. You know, a silent invitation."

Brody's lips twitched.

Damn. He'd been so focused on remembering what it tasted like, how it'd felt, he'd forgotten all the other reasons he liked that mouth of hers.

All the more reason not to invite her in.

"Why are you here?"

"Oh, look. He speaks," she said in a cheery tone, lifting one hand to the empty yard as if inviting the worms and bugs to listen up.

Refusing to smile, Brody put on his most ferocious scowl. The one that made hard-ass recruits wish they were home hiding behind their momma.

Genna just smiled.

"I'm here for two reasons," she said in that irritatingly upbeat tone of hers. As if she really thought she could smile him out of his mood. "The first is an official welcome from Mayor Tucker, who would be honored if you'd join him one day this week for lunch."

Was she kidding?

Did he look like the kind of guy who did lunch?

Apparently asking herself that same question, Genna bit her lip and gave a frustrated sigh.

"I'm guessing from your excited expression that this invitation is the highlight of your week. But wait, I've got even more wonderful news."

She paused, giving him an expectant look. Brody just shifted, leaning his shoulder on the frame of the door so he could take his weight off the vicious throbbing in his leg.

"You know, I've been told I'm the best community outreach liaison this town has ever had. Now, granted, I'm the only one it's had, so there might be a little bias going on. But still, people are usually a little more impressed by my charm than you seem to be."

Oh, he was impressed by her charms, all right. He let his gaze wander again, enjoying the contrast of the vivid red sweater against her golden skin and the way her jeans molded her long legs.

Charming temptation. That was Genna.

"I'm not interested in company, cookies or invitations." He paused, then lied, "Of any kind."

Hurt flashed in her eyes for a second, assuring him that she'd gotten the message.

Good. He hated to waste his breath.

"I was hoping we could talk," she told him. She rounded her eyes and did a little head tilt thing, indicating the house behind her. "Your gramma asked me to."

He followed her gesture in time to see his grandmother's head disappear and the screen door shut. Nice. Gramma Irene was trying to save him with sugar—and he didn't mean the cookies.

"I thought you were the community outreach liaison here on the behest of the mayor."

"That, too."

Right.

"Not interested," he said again.

She huffed. Actually bunched one fist on her slender hip and gave a big huff. He wanted to grin but he figured it'd just give her crazy ideas.

He tilted his head toward the walkway instead, indicating she should go.

"C'mon, just five minutes. We'll ease your grandmother's worries and I'll be able to tell my boss I did my job." When his expression didn't change, she pouted.

He eyed the stubborn tilt of her chin. Another thing that apparently hadn't changed. It was as if the last ten years hadn't even happened.

It all crashed down on him.

Thanks to a bad leg, he was trapped in Bedford. Because of the mission that'd jacked his leg, his life sucked and he had no freaking hope for the future.

And here was Genna, the town princess. Shining bright and cheery. The sexiest thing he'd ever seen.

He gritted his teeth against the pain of it all.

She'd gotten him in trouble once before.

For his first year in the navy, he'd cursed her walking into that garage. But even as he cursed, he hadn't been able to regret it. Hell, he was already paying the price. What was the point of not enjoying the memory?

By his second year, he realized she'd inadvertently saved him. A girl like Genna was out of reach for a guy like him. An impossible dream that he wasn't stupid enough to think he'd had a chance at keeping. But because he'd touched that dream, he'd found a shot at a great life. At a life he was great at.

And now? Now it was all gone.

Despair poured over him like tar, black, sticky and impossible to ignore. Damn Genna for making him open the door, both to the guesthouse and to the past.

Done with the conversation, and all the emotions it stirred up, he turned away. Two excruciating steps, even though he tried not to put too much weight on his leg, and he let the door swing shut behind him.

With Genna on the other side where she belonged.

He closed his eyes, leaning his head back, and sighed when he heard the door *snick* back open.

He should have known.

"Brody, please, listen to me."

"I told you to go," he said, not turning around.

"Not until we talk."

God, was there no end to the woman's stubborn streak?

She still hadn't learned when to give it up. And why should she? She wasn't the one who'd paid for playing with fire.

He was.

Not because he'd been shanghaied into the navy. But because once there, he'd found himself. He'd found his path, his life. He'd made a difference, for himself, for his country. And now it was gone. Freaking blown to hell like his leg, and as dead as his friend.

And here she was, doing it again. Those big blue eyes gleaming with an invitation that spelled trouble. The delicious, mind-numbing, body-draining kind of trouble that made a man stupid.

Tempting him, stirring up longings and hopes that had no chance in hell of surviving.

Playing with a sweet thing like Genna could only end up with the same results as last time.

A glimpse of heaven, a little bit of delight and yeah, sure, probably a little happiness. But it wouldn't last. Nothing did.

And when it was done?

He'd be right back where he started, alone and empty.

With yet another memory of what he couldn't have.

Hadn't he paid enough already?

He had nothing left.

6

"CAN'T YOU TAKE A HINT?" he asked gruffly, turning around in time to see her set the cookies on a small table by the door. "Even when the hint is spelled out in short, simple words."

"I'll go in a minute. Right after I pass on the messages I'm supposed to." She put on that obstinate look he remembered so well, chin high and arms crossed over her chest. Fine. She wanted to see stubborn, he'd show her a thing or two.

He didn't say a word. Instead he crossed the room— what should be a quick task given that it was the size of his footlocker but was instead a study in pain. Genna's eyes got wider with every step closer he took.

Unfortunately, his body got harder with each step, too.

By the time he was standing next to her, his head was filled with her scent. Sweet spice, it wrapped around him like a warm hug that quickly turned hot.

He was trained to control his body. To ignore pain, to push through discomfort. He'd endured Hell Week. He'd trekked eight miles through a jungle in Bolivia once with a broken ankle. He'd won five hundred bucks once betting that he could sit through three hours of Farrelly brothers without cracking a smile.

But the scent of Genna's hair made him quiver. Sent his head into a tailspin and his body into overdrive.

He told himself to resist. Warned his body not to engage.

His body ignored the warning. It was as if she was jamming his radar and manipulating the signals.

He didn't like it.

"What do you really want, Genna?" he asked, furious at the frustration coursing through his system. Frustration that was all her fault, dammit. He'd been fine holed up here, ignoring the world and reliving every miserable detail of the end of his last mission. The explosion. The helplessness.

The memories gripped him with inky black fingers, trying to pull him down. But Genna's big eyes, sexy mouth and intoxicating scent held his attention, forcing him to stay in the here and now.

"I told you, the mayor asked me to stop by." She bit her lip, studying his face as if she were gauging just how much to share of the rest of the mayor's wants. "He wanted to extend his appreciation for your service."

Smart girl, she'd realized it was pointless to repeat the stupid luncheon idea. Brody narrowed his gaze when Genna looked away, her fingers twining together before she tucked them into the front pockets of her jeans. Clearly there was something else she hadn't mentioned. Whatever it was, he didn't care. The idea of him and the mayor having lunch was ridiculous. Ten years ago, Tucker had been just starting out as the county's assistant D.A., with a lot of ambition and an oft-shared goal of getting losers like Brody off the streets.

"I don't serve for appreciation," he said, his tone gruffer than he'd intended.

Genna opened her mouth, that full lower lip glistening with temptation. Then she snapped it shut and shrugged. He'd like to think that meant she was done and would leave, but he was starting to realize that she had a stubborn streak wider than his own.

"Your grandmother is worried about you. If you don't want to meet with the mayor and discuss getting a little of the recognition you deserve, fine. But at least talk to your gramma." She lifted both hands in the air, the gesture matching the exasperation on her face. "Why did you come home if you were only going to hide out?"

Good question.

Brody's scowl deepened when he couldn't come up with an answer.

"Time to go." He reached out, wrapping his hand around her arm to turn her in the direction of the door. But the move put pressure on his bad leg so he had to shift his weight to compensate. And ended up way too close to Genna.

Close enough to feel her body heat.

Close enough that her scent, teasing before, grabbed him in a choke hold, not letting go.

Close enough that he could see the darker rings of blue around her pupils, could see the individual lashes that made up the lush fringe around her eyes.

He yanked his hand away.

"If you wanted, maybe we could go to lunch instead." Her words were low and husky with curiosity, her eyes hinting at nerves and something more. Something that grabbed at Brody, made him want the impossible. "If you just needed someone to talk to, someone to help you deal with all the emotional stuff you're facing, I'm a good listener."

"You want to have lunch and talk?" he asked, sure he'd heard her wrong. "About my emotions?"

"If that's what you wanted."

Hell, no. He didn't talk missions, he didn't talk about the military. And he sure as hell didn't talk about emotions.

Brody pressed his fingers against his temple, trying to rub away the tangle she was making of his thoughts.

"You should talk to someone, Brody. Your gramma, me, anyone. You're hurt and you're back in Bedford for the first time since you left. That has to mean something." She paused, taking a deep breath that made him want to slide his lips along her collarbone, then she reached out. Her fingers came within millimeters of touching his arm, but didn't make contact. It was as if she was testing the electrical charge between them, seeing how potent it was.

The hairs on his arm stood up, his entire body reacting as if she'd slid those fingers over him. Touching, soft and gentle, everywhere.

"I don't talk," he said, irritated that the words were mellow, not abrupt.

"Not even about our night?" She gave a tiny wince, as if she knew she'd crossed a line. Then, typical of the Genna he remembered, now that she'd crossed it, she danced all over the other side. "I never forgot it."

"You need to leave." He'd said the words to her so many times, they were like a catchphrase now.

"Brody—"

No. He couldn't deal with this now. Not her, not the memories. Not the feelings she was stirring up.

"Don't make me do something you'll regret," he warned quietly.

For a second, Genna stilled.

Then, damn her, she gave a soft little laugh and pressed her hand against his chest. Not to push him away. Simply to touch.

Her fingers burned his flesh, fired his needs.

"You won't hurt me," she said quietly, the absolute confidence in her tone baffling. Did she really trust him that much? Did she have no clue the things he'd done, the things he'd seen?

"I won't have to hurt you."

There were so many other things he could do to her. With her. On her and under her.

Her letters, always there tucked away in a private corner of his mind, surfaced. The door he'd slammed shut flew open, giving him access he hadn't allowed himself since his last mission.

The memories of those letters were a reward, a treat. Special. Something he'd enjoyed as he reveled in how freaking awesome his life was. The words played through his mind. The images of caramel, pulsating water and blue silk all crashed together in his brain in a huge, horny wave of need.

He wasn't interested in need, though.

He just wanted to be left alone. Physically, and mentally.

As always, he used the tools at hand to win the battle. He didn't go for guilt himself, but that didn't mean he didn't know how to wield it with laser precision.

It was only fair that he give her one last warning before he moved in.

"We're done. You delivered your invites. I turned them down. Time to go." His tone was low, menacing. He shifted his weight just enough, pulling back his shoulders and angling his chin so he loomed over her.

Intimidating.

She swallowed loud enough for him to hear her teeth click. Her pulse raced. He could see it thrumming in her throat. But her expression didn't change. She just kept looking at him with that cheerful smile and calm eyes.

Damn, she was something.

And *something* was the last thing he needed in his life right now.

WELL, THIS WASN'T going very well. Genna didn't know what she'd thought would happen when she talked to Brody. She hadn't let herself imagine that far, figuring the reality was going to be so much better than anything she'd imagined.

Disappointment sat hard and tight in her belly.

She hadn't let herself imagine what it would be like. But she'd entertained a few worries about what she'd hoped it wouldn't. Like that he'd be holding a grudge for that night before he'd left for the navy. Or that he'd be involved with someone, possibly serious. Or maybe that he'd only see her as Joe's little sister and want to talk about her brother.

Turns out she hadn't worried nearly enough. She needed to work on that.

"You're not leaving." His statement was so matter-of-fact, it was as though he was simply accepting the inevitable.

Genna wanted to smile, to pretend they could move on to rebuilding—okay, building outside of her imagination—their relationship. But she wasn't stupid. Right beneath his calm words was a whole lot of anger and nothing that invited building anything except space between them.

She should leave. She knew she should, but she was so afraid if she walked out this door, that'd be it. Her last, her only chance to talk to Brody, to find out what'd happened after that night. To discover how he felt about her…

Her fingernails cut into the soft flesh of her palms as she debated. Run or stay. Smart or stupid.

Then Brody moved and took the choice away.

"You ever been warned not to play with fire? Not to poke a sleeping tiger? Not to take candy from strangers?"

Despite his serious tone, her lips twitched.

"I'm not playing, I'm talking. You're awake. And I brought you cookies, not the other way around. You're welcome to offer me candy, though. I like peanut butter M&M's best."

His eyes lit for a second, then he shifted closer. His expression was hard, making her doubt the flash of humor she'd seen. She tried to step back, but realized he had her back against the wall next to the door.

He was only inches away.

So close she could smell his soap, clean and fresh, and see every detail of the stubble covering his chin. A couple days' worth, she realized, her hand aching to rub it and see if it was soft or rough.

Her gaze shifted, meeting Brody's eyes. His stare was intense, as if he were looking into her soul and figuring out all of her secrets. What he planned to do with them was what worried her, though.

"You should listen to good advice. And warnings." He leaned in closer, not touching her yet, but making her feel as if his hands were sweeping every inch of her body. "You never know when ignoring them will get you into trouble."

Genna's heart raced so fast, she swore she could feel it vibrating under her skin. Her body went into meltdown, needy and wanting more. It'd been so long since he'd touched her. Since he'd kissed her. Was it as good as she remembered? Was he better now?

She didn't care how stupid it was. She wanted to find out.

So when he leaned closer, his expression pure intimidation, frown and all, she leaned, too.

Right into his lips.

Oh. Her head spun, slow and intoxicating. Her body almost melted, he felt so good. She'd have thought that frown would make his lips hard. But no. They were soft. Welcoming.

Yummy.

Afraid to move, afraid to close her eyes, Genna stared up at Brody. Waiting.

Her heart raced, anticipation pounding through her veins. Surely he wouldn't turn her away. Would he? As he stood, rock-still, disappointment started to edge out the anticipation. Genna sighed against his mouth, preparing to move away and begin her descent into humiliated horror.

Then he took over.

He grabbed her arms, just above the elbow, lifting her higher so her toes barely brushed the floor. His mouth shifted, angling. Taking. His tongue plunged, dark and demanding as it drove deep into her mouth.

Genna's head fell back, giving him control. Giving him anything.

Her breath came in pants, her mind swirling with sensations even as the intensity of their kiss worked its magic on the rest of her body.

He was voracious.

His mouth took hers as if he were starving and she a feast, there to feed his every need. She'd never been kissed like this. Never felt this edge between passion and fury.

That he was angry was clear.

At her? At himself? At the situation? That part was up for grabs.

It didn't matter. She was sure she could soothe the anger with a few kisses. That she could reach inside and fix whatever made him so sad.

She shifted closer. Not quite plastering her body against his—she wasn't sure where his injury was and didn't want to hurt him. But close enough to feel the heat radiating off his body. To brush his chest with the tips of her breasts, sensitive even through the nubby knit of her sweater.

When she moved, his kiss changed. He pulled back, his lips softer now. Distant. Afraid he was going to end their kiss, she called up all of her nerve, wrapped her hands around the back of his neck to hold him in place and plunged her tongue into his mouth.

It was like flipping a switch.

No more anger. No more distance.

Just passion. Pure and sweet.

His tongue slid along hers and his hands wrapped around her waist under her sweater. Flesh against flesh. She shivered at the feel of his fingers, rough and strong against her skin.

His palm closed over her breast, making her whimper. It felt so good. Her nipples ached with a delicious kind of pain, so hard she was surprised they didn't rip her silk bra.

"More," she breathed against his mouth.

"Is this what you want?" he asked, his hand pressing between her thighs, the seam of her jeans riding against the swollen flesh and driving her crazy. "Is this how you want it?"

She'd rather have it naked, but she was too far gone to speak. She wasn't positive she was even breathing. All she could do was feel the amazing sensations rocketing through her body.

His fingers scraped over the seam of her jeans again, making her whimper. The sensations intensified, her entire body feeling like it was electrified. Desire coiled, tighter and tighter between her thighs. His lips closed over hers, tongue plunging before he lured hers into his mouth and sucked.

She exploded with a tiny whimper. Tiny sparks of light blew to pieces behind her closed eyes and the room spun as the orgasm poured through her. He slowed the kiss, then as her pants became shuddering breaths, trailed his lips over her cheek to bury his face in the crook of her neck.

Genna sighed, feeling as though she'd run a marathon.

In her jeans.

Again.

The guy had given her the two best orgasms of her life, and she hadn't gotten her jeans off for either of them.

Time to change that.

But suddenly, she was nervous.

This wasn't Brody, her brother's friend.

He was different now.

He'd seen things, done things that were beyond her comprehension. He was a soldier. A SEAL. The best of the best at doing the impossible.

Since there was nothing impossible about what she wanted him to do to her, this should be a piece of cake.

As if he'd read her thoughts, he slowly pulled back. Genna ran her palm over his cheek, smiling and ready to make a joke.

But the distance on his face was a little off-putting.

She took a shaky breath, trying to calm her racing heart.

She'd never felt this way before. Her body was still humming and she was ready to strip naked and do all the things to his body that she'd dreamed of for years. Things she'd had zero interest in doing to other guys' bodies. Brody things.

"You need to go," he growled. "Now. Before this goes too far."

Go? Was he kidding? The climax was still working its magic on her body in delightful little shudders.

"I think it needs to go just a little bit further," she corrected softly, nibbling kisses along his jaw and down his throat. He gave a low moan when she got to that spot beneath his ear, emboldening her. One hand still gripping his biceps for balance, she grazed the other down his side and across his rock-hard abs, taking a second to give her own moan of appreciation. Then, still nibbling, she slipped her fingers beneath the elastic waistband of his sweatpants.

Before she could explore, or even touch anything interesting, his hand shot out and grabbed her wrist.

"Further," she whispered in his ear, dipping her tongue along the rim before adding, "Please."

"Genna—"

"C'mon," she cajoled. "Let's see how good we are together. This is it, finally we get to give us a chance before you have to go back to being a big, bad SEAL heroically saving the world. Let's do it now."

It was as though the hard, hot body in her arms had turned to ice. She pulled back to look at him, trying to figure out what was going on.

"I'm not a damned hero," he ground out.

Genna laughed. "Of course you are. Even the president says so."

"I'm no hero and there is no we," he said with a laugh so bitter it made her mouth hurt. When Genna shook her head, he shifted aside. As if moving away from her body would make the differences between them all the more obvious. Since he was hard and she was panting, it was a smart strategy.

Genna wanted to thump her hand against her chest to force some air past the knot in her throat.

He was so big, looming over her. His body was like a solid wall of muscles. Even through his T-shirt, she could see them bunch, hard and firm beneath the fabric.

"Brody—" she said slowly, then went silent. She had no idea what to say. This wasn't the Brody she'd held in her mind all these years. The one she remembered as her gallant hero, the one who wrote her incendiary letters. The one who made her melt with just a look. Okay, maybe he was that last one, but not the rest. And she wasn't sure what to think about it.

"Look, we should—"

"No," he interrupted. "There is no we. There's you, the pampered princess. And there's me."

He paused, giving her a once-over that made her go hot and cold both at the same time. "Not interested."

Despite her confusion and the sick feeling in her stomach, hot passion was still gripping her limbs and pooling between her thighs. Genna dropped her eyes to the very large, very visible proof pressing against his sweatpants.

"No? You look mighty interested to me," she taunted without thinking. As soon as the words were out, though, she wished she could pull them back.

"Sweetheart, you want to get naked and do me right? Fine, let's go. I'm willing to let you. But that's not interest. That's over the minute I roll off your body."

His words hit Genna like a kick in the gut. Swift, well aimed and brutally painful. Emotionally reeling, she tried to take a breath, but it hurt so much.

"But I thought—" She broke off, not about to admit what their letters had meant to her. Or what these kisses were a sign of. And definitely not a peep about the fantasies, the dreams and the hopes she'd built around him over the years.

"You thought what? That because we played the old-school version of sexting that there was something going on? That because I'm willing to do you against the wall, it's special?"

Ouch. Genna frowned, suddenly feeling very naive. Apparently they taught mind reading in SEAL school.

"I didn't think the letters were a secret code for *let's run away together*. But neither did I think they were your version of a girl in every port." Wishing she were anywhere but here, Genna tried to ignore the tight knot of misery in her stomach, where only moments ago had been white-hot desire. "Did you write me just to be mean? For some kind of revenge? Is that what this was all about?"

For a second Brody looked as if he was going to protest. Then his expression smoothed again, back to stoic military machine.

"A day where we learn something isn't a day wasted," he told her in a sanctimonious tone that made her want to kick him in the shin. And not the good one.

"Well, I guess today is fabulous," Genna said, tears burning her eyes. She lifted her chin, daring them to fall. "I learned that you weren't the man I thought you were. I found out that you make an excellent bully and that you have no problem playing games and deliberately hurting someone."

She waited for him to protest. To claim she was wrong.

She wanted, desperately, for him to be that guy she'd always thought he was. To be the one who fought the odds, faced down the bullies. The one who protected her. That Brody was her hero.

But this one? His expression didn't change. She struggled to accept that this was the real him. The boy she'd known was a distant loner with a rough reputation and a questionable attitude. But she'd always been sure that was just a defense mechanism, maybe because his father sucked and he'd had such a bad childhood. On their night together he'd joked, he'd smiled. He'd been so sweet.

"But then, you've never known me, have you?"

Again with the mind reading. Genna wasn't sure if she wanted to cry, or to throw cookies at him. It wasn't as though she'd spent the last decade waiting around for him. But still, their relationship had been a cherished memory, that one thing that'd always made her feel special. Made her feel as if whatever else was lousy in her life, the hottest guy she'd ever crushed on had cared enough about her, about her reputation, to give up his freedom.

But it looked as though she was the only person who gave a damn about that memory.

Humiliation washed over her, making her blink fast to clear the burning from her eyes.

"I guess I don't know you. Not any better than anyone else around here. You're either the badass troublemaker son of the town drunk. Or maybe you're the abused grandson of a sweet lady who thinks you need saving. Or, wait, I know," she snapped, "you're the big bad hero the mayor wants to honor for your incredible service to your country. But whatever you are, it's not what I thought."

"Well, then," he said slowly, his words like gravel. "I guess that says it all. Maybe now you'll go?"

It wasn't his words that broke her heart, though. It was the look in his eyes. For one brief second, so much pain and loss flashed in those gold depths that she didn't know how he could survive it.

Genna didn't remember leaving the guesthouse. She wasn't sure if she ran across the alley, went around the house or sprouted wings and flew into her bedroom window.

She'd thought he'd forgiven her.

She'd thought he was interested in her, that those letters had meant something. That maybe he wanted her. The real her, not the perfectly behaved, please-everyone princess he'd so accurately dubbed her.

She'd thought they had something special between them. That those letters, that one night, they were proof of the passion and connection they shared.

Genna pressed her lips together, trying to stop the tears that were trailing, fiery hot, down her cheeks.

Now she was afraid he was a stranger.

One who hated her.

7

THERE WERE TIMES, miserable times, that a girl needed work. When it was good to have a job to focus on, to serve as a distraction from heartbreak.

This was not one of those times.

Real life sucked when she didn't have her secret fantasy to fall back on. After her mind-blowing climax, a nasty descent into reality and the proceeding all-night crying binge, Genna had tasked herself with getting over Brody. It shouldn't be that hard to get over a hero who had never existed, should it?

Three days later and she still hadn't figured out how. But hey, she had the rest of her long, lonely, dull life to work on it. She'd get there eventually.

She arranged coffee cups on a tray, making sure to add sugar in the form of cubes, granulated and raw. Yet another pathetic example of how sad her life was when the highlight of her day was getting the exact same amount of sugar in each bowl. It was enough to make her scream. Or maybe that was because her boss was still talking about his new favorite subject. Hometown Hero, Brody Lane.

"This event will be fabulous. We need to be sure enough press is invited. Not just lifestyle. I want current events, politics. War Hero Welcomed Home by Loving Town With Parade. That'll make a great headline."

"It needs work," Marcus Reilly said from his spot at the opposite end of the table from the mayor. "You're putting up a lot of fuss over a guy who, what? Did his job?"

Glad her back was to them, Genna freely rolled her eyes. *Did his job?* Leave it to her father to be a little black rain cloud. The sheriff had never been what anyone could call effusive. But over the last few years, the worse Joe's behavior was, the more withdrawn their father became. Almost as if he'd been expecting Joe's death and had figured on getting in some mourning ahead of time.

"Fine. We'll let the papers come up with the headline. Either way, hometown hero appreciation is good PR. A parade is good commerce and after all, it is election season," Tucker pointed out, those words saying it all.

The cookies arranged just so and coffee balanced on the tray, Genna turned toward the men gathered around the long teak table. An informal monthly meeting among Bedford's movers and shakers included the mayor and sheriff, of course. A couple of high-profile businesspeople, the bank owner and, she sighed, one perfect lawyer rounded up this month's powwow.

Avoiding the lawyer, Perfect Stewart who was still angling for a second date, she moved to the other side of the room with her tray. She wasn't sure how her job as community liaison had come to include playing hostess. But given that her job was more a backroom agreement between her boss and her father, she figured the mayor was looking for whatever he could to justify her paycheck. She'd protested the job once, wanting to quit and find something that she'd love. But that night Joe had been hauled in by Highway Patrol on drug charges. Her father had left midprotest to deal with the fallout. By the time he'd bailed out her brother, smoothed over the furor and glossed away the damage to his sheriff's reputation, Genna had given up arguing.

"Coffee?" she asked the room at large as she set the tray in the center of the table. Then she stepped back, returning to the counter to prepare the backup plate of cookies she knew they'd want soon.

It was bad enough she had to hostess these things. She drew the line at being waitress. As appreciative sounds and compliments on the cookies started flowing around the table, she admitted she didn't mind playing caterer, though.

Besides, she'd been on a baking binge for the last four days, ever since her encounter with Brody. Every counter in her kitchen was covered in some treat or another. And that was after sharing with all of her neighbors, her friends and the senior center.

"Genna?" Mayor Tucker called around a mouthful of cookie. "Have you spoken to Lane again? Has he agreed to meet with me?"

Go back and see Brody? The man who made her insides melt, turned her body into a panting puddle of passion and then summarily rejected her?

No, no and hell, no. Genna tried to think of a polite way to reword that. Before she could, her father gave a garbled protest.

"What? You sent Genna to talk to him?" The sheriff straightened, his cookie crumbs blasting across the table. His face turned a worrying shade of red and his mouth worked as if he was chewing up words to keep from spitting them out.

Looks of shock and worry flew around the room.

"Of course," the mayor said slowly. "That's her job."

Genna's face heated. Unspoken, but heard loud and clear by everyone in the room, was that it was a job her father had actively solicited, then called on all his parental guilt pressure to get her to take.

"I don't want her near Lane. The guy is a loser."

It was too much. He decided her job. He tried to control her dating. And now he was railroading her boss as to what her duties were? Anger bubbled up, slow at first but rapidly heating.

Forgetting her desire to stay as far away from Brody as possible, Genna stepped forward to argue. Both against her father's high-handed mandate as he continued to try to run her life, and at the idea that Brody was a loser.

Thankfully before she got a word out, and caused a scene that would send her father into yet another meltdown and her mother to the hospital to have her heart checked, someone cleared their throat.

"Brody Lane?" Stewart asked, confusion clear on his face. "The guy we're planning a parade for? The navy SEAL recently recommended for a Silver Star?" He let the words hang in the room for a few seconds, then gave a baffled shake of his head. "That guy is a loser?"

"No, no," Tucker broke in, giving the sheriff a quick glare before plastering over it with a cheesy smile. "That's old history. Sheriff Reilly remembers when Brody Lane was a troubled teen, well before the U.S. Navy turned him around. It's quite a rags-to-riches story. Something to include in the article, don't you think?"

"Get him yourself, then. Genna's not going near the guy."

Holy crap, she was sick of men. Sick of them deciding what she could or should do. Sick of them treating her as if she couldn't make her own decisions, or if she did, of them proving to her just how stupid some of those decisions might be.

"I'm standing right here," she pointed out in her chilliest tone. "If you want me to do something, or would rather I didn't, why don't you tell me directly?"

"This doesn't concern you, Genna," her father said dismissively.

Genna's jaw dropped. It wasn't her reaction that goaded her father into recanting, though. It was the expressions on the rest of the faces in the room.

"What I mean is that protecting the citizens of Bedford is my job, and this is part of that," he said, giving Genna a paternal look. The kind a proud father gives a little kid, loving and indulgent and just a little patronizing.

It made Genna want to throw a tantrum just to justify it.

But the minute she snapped, the family drama would start. Guilt, games, hospital trips. Every freaking time.

Her throat closed up and black dots danced in front of her vision. Genna felt as if she was choking. It was all she could do to breathe, which was probably just as well given the words that were trying to trip off her tongue.

Finally, she sucked in a deep breath, lifted her chin and gave her father a chilly smile.

"I guess you don't need me, then, do you?"

Ignoring the uncomfortable looks ricocheting around the room, Genna packed up the rest of her cookies. They'd all gotten a big old dose of gossip fodder. They weren't feasting on her baking, too.

The last thing she heard as she swept through the door with all the majesty of the princess title Brody had pinned on her was her father's muttered words.

"I'm gonna kick Brody Lane's ass."

BRODY STOOD BY the small lake down the hill from the park, noting that the cattails were chest-high now and the surrounding trees had created a canopy overhead. He used to come down here with his buddies after dark to drink. Or, every once in a while, with a girl, since not much action could be had on the backseat of a Harley. Some enterprising kid had tied a rope to one branch, right above the no-swimming sign.

Bet the local law loved that.

He missed the ocean.

He missed activity.

Hell, he missed reveille, spot inspections and mess hall chow.

"So this is where you're hiding?"

Brody sighed.

What he didn't miss were people. Which was one of the reasons he'd chosen this side of the park. It was rarely populated.

"If I was hiding, you wouldn't be able to find me." He didn't turn around when he said it, just kept staring at the murky water.

"You don't look surprised to see me," Masters said as he reached Brody's side, mimicking his stance of both hands in his pockets staring over the lake.

"I heard you stomping down the path." And he'd been expecting him. Irene had passed on a half dozen phone messages, each one more demanding than the last. Brody had ignored them, of course. But nobody put Masters off for long. If the guy wasn't so brilliant, his call sign would be Bulldog instead of Genius.

"I came to haul you out of hiding."

"I'm not hiding. I'm recovering." Brody gestured to the uneven path. "Walking, working the kinks out, pushing my limits."

"Moseying through a cozy small-town park at dusk pushes your limits?"

Brody shrugged.

Leaving the house pretty much pushed his limits these days.

"The doctor's report said you're ready for PT. Actually, I'm paraphrasing a little. What it said is that you should have reported to base to start thrice-weekly physical therapy a week ago, as soon as you got back to California."

"I'm on leave."

"Convalescent leave. Which, according to the manual, means you're off duty but still obligated to fulfill your duties, such as they are laid out by your superior officer."

"You read too much."

"We've all got our faults." Masters shrugged, kicking around the rocks and gravel beneath their feet.

"I figured I'd take another few days. Start physical therapy next week," Brody said. Not really a lie. If he'd thought about it at all, he'd definitely have put it off.

"Why?"

Brody hunched his shoulders, glaring at the water and wishing he'd opted for a nice, anonymous hotel room in some remote city to recuperate. Masters still would have found him, but it'd have taken the guy a couple extra hours.

"I'm not ready."

His teammate was silent for a few seconds, still stirring the rocks with his foot as if searching for gold. He bent down, grabbed a flat rock and sent it skipping over the lake. Three bounces. Not bad.

"PTSD?"

"I jacked up my leg," Brody snapped. "Not my head."

"Dude, that mission went straight to hell. Landon is still chewing on asses over the intelligence breakdown. And you bore the brunt of it. Nobody'd think less of you if you were having trouble processing it. There's no shame in that."

Brody puffed out a breath. He wasn't dissing guys facing it. Post-traumatic stress disorder was real, and from what he'd seen, it was pure hell. He thought about pointing out that he'd gotten through debriefing just fine, but he knew Masters wouldn't buy that. Debriefing didn't mean jack. Guys came back from missions, left the military all the time with their heads inside out. A guy didn't do or see the kind of things SEALs did without it taking a toll.

"I'm not ashamed. I'm just saying that's not the issue."

"Then you'll report for physical therapy tomorrow."

He quickly marshaled a handful of arguments. His bike was on base, so he didn't have wheels. His right leg was damaged, not in any shape to operate a car. And he couldn't ask his sweet little gramma to drive him the two-hour commute back and forth to Coronado. He wasn't even sure she had a license anymore.

He didn't offer up any of them, though. SEALs didn't make excuses.

"You could consider it an order," Masters said in a contemplative tone, bending down to pick up another stone, then winging it across the lake.

Brody grimaced. Not that the guy scored five bounces. But that he'd resort to pulling rank.

"Deal with whatever's going on. You need someone to talk to, give me a yell. But don't take forever. The team is waiting for you to finish this little vacation and get your ass back to work." Masters waited a beat, then added, "Besides, we miss your cookies. Can you get your gramma to send a care package with you when you come in tomorrow?"

Brody snorted.

Then, straightening his shoulders, he faced reality as he had so many times in the past. Orders were orders, no matter how ugly they were or what degree of reluctance he felt about them. He'd do PT until reevaluation. What he did afterward, well, time would tell.

"You need a ride?"

"Waste of resources," Brody pointed out, thinking of the car that'd dropped him off from the airport.

"Dude, we're on leave. The team will take turns playing taxi until the doctor green-lights you on your bike. Or you could rent something safe. A Smart Car, maybe."

Brody laughed, turning to face Masters for the first time since his buddy had joined him. The guy looked good. Normal, except for the seven stitches holding his cheek together. They'd all taken a hit on that mission.

But Brody had been the last man out. Well, second to last. His smile dropped, Carter's face flashing in his mind just before the guy had gone flying through the air.

"You okay?"

Brody blinked, then shrugged.

"Other than being ordered to see some dumbass who's gonna play with my body? Yeah, I'm fine."

After a long, narrow-eyed inspection, Masters nodded and turned to go.

"Don't forget the cookies," he called over his shoulder.

Brody let his mind go blank. It was a lot easier than facing the questions Masters's visit had planted in his mind. Questions that'd been there already, nicely buried. Thanks to his buddy, they'd made their ugly way to the surface. Much harder to ignore.

But not impossible.

The sun was sliding low when he finally made his way up the hill. He wanted to blame the chilly weather for the stiffness in his leg and pain shooting from ankle to shoulder.

He'd just cleared the hill, beads of sweat coating his forehead with an icy chill. He hunched his shoulders and ignored the pain.

"Hold it right there," growled a familiar voice.

Brody's fists clenched in his pockets, his jaw tight to hold back the cusswords.

Was there a beacon that went off whenever he cleared the lake? How many times in his life had this guy busted him right here, in this very spot?

And what the hell was with today? Had he missed the note on the calendar calling it face-your-demons day? First Masters with the reminders of the mission. Now Reilly was here to throw off the careful barriers Brody had slammed around any thoughts of Genna. Or more particularly, of the piss-poor way he'd treated her.

His attitude slid downward, from rotten to pure crap. He forced himself to pull it back. It'd been ten years. He was too old to play rebel badass. Besides, he'd made his peace with the sheriff's actions years ago. No point in holding a grudge.

"Lane." Reilly gave him a once-over, his tone as cool as the look on his face. "You have a reason for being here?"

Looked like time didn't do a damned thing to blunt other people's grudges.

"Walking is against the law?"

"I see the service didn't do anything about that smart mouth of yours."

"Actually, it improved it. Nobody swears or smarts off with the same finesse as a sailor."

Reilly just stared. Cold, with layers of anger that said he'd be more than happy to take off his badge and kick Brody's smart ass.

Brody grinned, amused for the first time in weeks.

Did the guy actually think he was intimidating? Brody had been stared down, shot at and ordered about by hard-asses that made Sheriff Reilly look like a cute little pussy-cat.

"Stay away from my daughter."

What? Had Genna run to Daddy, complaining that the big mean guy had kissed her?

Brody's grin slid away.

He made a show of looking left, then right. Then, just to prod the guy a little further, he glanced behind him before offering the sheriff a shrug.

"I don't seem to be anywhere near your daughter."

"Clearly the navy didn't teach you respect," Reilly muttered, resting his hand on the butt of his pistol. What, like he thought that'd get him the quote-unquote respect he apparently wanted?

Since Brody could have that weapon out of the guy's possession and neutralized in twenty seconds—an extra ten because he was injured and hadn't trained in a couple of months—he was having trouble finding the will to be intimidated.

Nor was he finding any for this conversation.

Before, the highlight of his discussions with the good sheriff was to see how far he could push the guy. To find each particular button and give it a good jab.

Now, he just didn't care.

"You looked me up for a reason, Sheriff. Why don't you get to it so we can both be on our way?"

Reilly blinked, then frowned. His hand shifted to his belt as he gave Brody a searching look.

"I told you, stay away from Genna."

"I haven't gone looking for your daughter."

"But you've seen her."

No point denying the truth. But neither was Brody stupid enough to fill in any blanks, either. Instead he just waited.

"Genna's not smart enough to know when she's being taken for a ride," the sheriff said, for the first time looking like a concerned father instead of an uptight cop. "She's got some starry-eyed idea that you're a hero. Same way she thinks drunks are safe to talk to and that her brother was gonna rehabilitate."

Brody rocked back on his heels, his mind adjusting to the lineup he'd just joined. Drunks and a prison-shivved junkie. Talk about perspective. The kind that grated down his spine. But as much as it killed him to let it slide, he didn't take the bait.

"Sounds to me like the person you need to talk to is your daughter," he said instead.

"I'll be talking to her. But I'm warning you, too. She's vulnerable, and not good at seeing through bullshit. Naive and easily confused."

Were they talking about the same woman? Genna Reilly, leggy spitfire with a wicked mouth and an attitude that didn't quit? Did the guy know his daughter at all?

"She's spent a lot of years getting her life on the straight and narrow, and keeping it there. She doesn't need any bad influences dragging her off."

"When did Genna fall off the straight and narrow?" Like the man's earlier one, this image simply didn't compute. Genna might be pure temptation wrapped in bold sassiness, but she was still the epitome of the town sweetheart.

"The only reason she didn't go the same way as her brother is because her mother and I kept a tighter rein on her. Kept her away from influences like you, made sure she works the right job, lives in the right place."

In other words, they'd tucked her under their thumb and hadn't let go.

Damn.

Brody felt like an ass. It was bad enough that he'd been a total jerk to her. Now to find out he'd only been act 1 in the ass brigade marching through her life.

He'd been fine justifying his treatment of Genna when it was only the two of them. But knowing her father was giving her shit for something she hadn't done seriously pissed him off.

"You've been warned," Sheriff Reilly snapped, turning to leave.

Brody wanted to hate the guy.

Still…

"Sheriff?"

Reilly stopped and looked over his shoulder.

"I'm sorry about Joe."

Grief-laced anger flashed, raw and painful in the older man's eyes for a second, then he blinked it away. He gave Brody another one of those searching looks, offered a silent nod and kept on walking.

Jerk.

Brody was still fuming when he got back to his hidey-hole of a house, his leg screaming protest at the extra pressure his stomp home had put on it.

For the first time, he looked past the guesthouse to the house on the other side of the alley. Lights glowed, the windows glistening against the darkening sky.

Then he glanced at the door of his hidey-hole.

Brody debated for all of three seconds.

Time to have a chat with Sheriff Reilly's little girl.

8

WHAT THE HELL was wrong with men?

Were they good for anything besides the occasional orgasm and spider removal?

"Genna, your mom called. Again."

"I'm not here."

Macy huffed in the kitchen doorway, then made her way into the bowels of temptation as she called it. Genna called it therapy. She looked around the counters covered in pies, cookies, cakes and her latest experiment, cookie-pops.

"You're gonna have to take her call," Macy said, her tone distracted as she stood a good foot away from the counter but leaning so close she was almost bent in half as she sniffed the coconut cake. "Otherwise she's going to send the EMT over again."

Focusing all her attention on the ziplocked bag of graham crackers she was crushing with a rolling pin, Genna just shrugged.

Since there was no impact in sending the cops, given that Genna's dad headed up that game, Cara Reilly had taken to calling for an ambulance when her daughter ignored her. After all, the only reason Genna could ever not respond was that she'd fallen in the shower, or slipped

down the staircase, or cut her head off while slicing to-
matoes.

Genna beat the bag so hard the seams exploded, sending graham cracker crumbs all over the counter. It was un-
thinkable that her daughter might not want to talk.

"If you talk to her, she'll quit calling," Macy said with
an impatient look.

"If I talk to her, I might actually need an EMT." Genna
swept the crumbs off the counter into her hand, her moves
jerky with irritation.

"What'd she do that's so bad?"

Genna shrugged and grabbed a paper towel to clean up
the mess instead of answering.

What was the point?

Macy didn't get it. She saw Genna's parents as poster-
perfect, the epitome of what every parent should be. At-
tentive, helpful and always there to offer advice on their
daughter's life. What she didn't see, or chose to ignore
since Genna had pointed it out a few million times, was
that they were smothering her.

"I'm going to stay at Greg's for a little while," Macy
finally said, sidling closer to a triple-layer coconut cream
cake and swiping a fingerful of frosting.

"Because my mother keeps calling?" Wow, maybe her
parents' nagging and interference had finally paid off.
Not that she didn't love Macy, but she was seriously tired
of justifying her mood, choices and entire freaking life.

"No. Because you keep baking. In the last three weeks,
you've made enough food to stock a fancy bakery. I can't
take it. I'd rather stay with Greg and risk a big fight before the wedding than stay here and ensure I can't fit in
my dress."

Genna winced. Shaking the cracker crumbs off her fingers, she finally turned to look at her friend.

Macy's face was creased with concern. Another reason

to leave, Genna supposed. No bride should have worry lines on her special day.

"I'm sorry," she murmured, glancing around the room and seeing what her friend probably saw. Holy cow. It did look like a bakery had relocated to her kitchen. "I have no idea what I'm going to do with all of this."

She'd been so focused on baking to avoid her thoughts, she hadn't considered what to do with the results.

Macy backed away as if the very question opened the door to the possibility of her eating it all. Then she stopped, sighed and scooped up another taste of coconut frosting.

"You won't burn yourself out before you need to make my wedding cake, will you?"

Genna laughed for the first time in three days. What was Macy going to obsess over after mid-May?

"Of course not. I love to bake. I can't imagine ever burning out on it." Of course, she hadn't been able to imagine her heart being stomped on and her dreams trampled while she was still quivering from a mind-blowing climax, either. So what did she know?

"Will you be okay here by yourself?"

"I'll be fine."

Better than fine, actually, since all she wanted right now was to be left alone. She didn't want to talk, she had no interest in sharing her heartbreak or hearing advice. And if Macy wasn't here, she could turn off the phone altogether. After putting in a call to the EMT center to let them know to ignore her mother, of course.

Nope, she'd rather be alone, baking and contemplating the useless dissatisfaction that was her life.

Fun, fun.

"Go, live with your fiancé," she said, shooing Macy out of the kitchen before she gave in to self-pity and changed her mind. "Have wild sex, play house, try togetherness on for size."

"Genna," Macy protested, blushing. "We don't have wild sex."

What was the point of getting married, then?

Not wanting to prolong the departure, Genna kept that question to herself. Instead, she wiped her hands and helped Macy carry a half dozen bags and boxes to the car. A quick wave, a few warnings and reminders to call her mom from Macy, and voilà.

Peace and quiet.

Exhausted but not willing to go to bed at—she glanced at the clock and winced—7:00 p.m.? Pissed off, miserable and frustrated made for an exhausting cocktail.

She stepped back into the kitchen and looked around.

It did look like she was stocking a bakery with goods.

Maybe she could set up a stand in the front yard. Three cookies for a dollar. A few hundred dozen and she might have enough money to afford a sheriff-approved storefront.

Playing with that dream, a nice distraction from her earlier thoughts, Genna returned to building her cheesecake crust. Butter, graham crackers, ground almonds. All yummy goodness.

She was entertaining the mental debate over decorating her dream bakery in modern teal and brown, or going with a fun black-and-pink palette when there was a rap at her back door. Loud enough to make her jump and almost drop the cream cheese. Her heart pounding just as loud now, she shifted to the side of the kitchen to look out the window.

Brody?

She blinked, moved closer to the window in case the porch light was casting illusions, then looked again.

Tall, sexy and gorgeous. Yep, that was Brody all right.

She scowled. What did he want?

She debated for all of three seconds before checking to see that the lock was engaged, then jaw set, took the cream cheese back to the mixer. When the knock came again, she flipped the mixer on high to drown it out.

"It's usually better to hide in another room if you're pretending not to be there when someone knocks."

Genna jumped, but managed to contain her scream. She was so proud, she gave herself a couple seconds for her heart to slow again before turning off the mixer. Had he learned lock-picking in SEAL school? Or was that a leftover from his badass days? Pasting on her most distant expression, she tossed a cool expression over her shoulder.

"It's usually better to take the hint. When someone doesn't answer the door it means they don't want to see you."

"I've never been good with subtleties."

No question about that. Brody and subtle didn't even belong in the same sentence. Genna pulled her gaze back to the creamy mixture in her bowl, wishing he didn't look so good. A quick glance told her he'd lost some of that pallor, the crisp evening air and scent of the outdoors adding to the healthy impression.

Too bad.

She'd been imagining him wasting away with guilt, miserable over having rejected her and pining away to nothing.

"Saw your old man tonight," he said, letting the door slam shut behind him. "So what's the deal? You tell your daddy I'm being mean to you?"

"Wow, not subtle or polite," she said, pretending to measure the vanilla instead of just pouring it into the bowl to give her face time to cool off. Damn her father.

"Genna?"

Pressing her lips together, she finally turned to him. And immediately crossed her arms over her chest. Both to keep her hands to herself, and to hide the instant evidence of her body's reaction.

He was so damned sexy.

His leather jacket did nothing to disguise the breadth of his shoulders, and instead of sweats he was in jeans tonight. Jeans that molded nicely to his hard thighs. Whew, it was hot in here.

"Well?"

Well, what? Did he want her to say it out loud? That he was gorgeous or that she went into instant meltdown just being in the same room as him.

Then she replayed the conversation and grimaced.

"I didn't say anything to my father. He was at the meeting when the mayor asked if I'd contacted you again. I said no, my father said never, I walked out. End of story."

Brows furrowed, Brody stared long enough to make her want to squirm. Then he nodded and looked around the room. His eyes got wider as they passed from counter to tabletop to counter.

He gave a baffled shake of his head. "Do you run your own bakery? Or are you supplying treats for the Fifth Fleet?"

Starting to get a baking complex and wondering if she should look into a twelve-step program, Genna followed his gaze and sighed.

Then, not willing to relax her guard since the minute she did all those schoolgirl dreams would come floating right back, Genna gave him an arch look.

"Why are you here?"

All the way in the room now, he was peering from tray to plate, then chose a butter pecan cookie and popped it into his mouth.

"I told you," he said around the cookie. "Your father came to see me."

"And told you I said you were mean?"

"Actually he warned me to stay the hell away from you."

Genna closed her eyes against the humiliation. She was twenty-seven and her father warned away guys he didn't like. Her mother called her three times a day and sicced emergency personnel on her if she didn't respond. Could her life be any more pathetic?

Forcing herself to meet his gaze again, she offered a stiff smile and a shrug.

"Okay. So he warned you. That shouldn't be a big deal since according to you, you don't want to be anywhere near me anyhow." She waited, but his expression didn't change. "So I'll ask again. Why are you here?"

"I told you. Because your father told me to stay away."

"Seriously? You're here to defy my father?"

"Sure." He shrugged. "Why not?"

Genna was pretty certain she wouldn't have been more shocked if he'd stripped naked and asked her to eat cookies off his body.

IT WAS ALL BRODY could do not to laugh.

The look on Genna's face was priceless. Baffled fury, coated in a pink wash of embarrassment.

She was adorable.

And he was pretty sure that was the first time in his life he'd ever used the word *adorable*.

The kitchen timer dinged. After a couple of blinks and a bewildered shake of her head, Genna grabbed a cloth and hurried to the oven. As soon as she opened it, a spicy rich scent filled the room. Giant cookies, the size of his hand and studded with chocolate, covered the tray. His mouth actually watered.

"Let me get this straight." She set the tray of cookies on the counter, opposite Brody and too far for him to sneak one. A frown between narrowed eyes, she gave him a long look. Strikingly similar to her father's look, actually. Brody's lips twitched. She probably wouldn't want to hear that.

"I write to give you bad news, and you hit on me by mail. I come to see you to pass on an invitation and a message—neither of which are from me—and you feel me up then kick me out. And today my father, clearly overstepping both his parental and legal bounds, warns you to stay away from me." She paused, as if waiting for him to dispute anything she'd said so far. Since she was pretty much on track, he just shrugged. "And now that I am, according to someone who has no say in it, off-limits, what? You want me?"

"I didn't say I wanted you," Brody corrected quickly. No point giving her the wrong idea. Or in this case, the right idea that he planned to ignore.

"Ah, my mistake." She tossed her hands in the air, the move sending the scent of fresh-baked cookies through the room. Brody's stomach growled. Risking her glare, and the spatula she was currently smacking against her palm, he snagged a cookie from the closest tray.

It melted in his mouth, rich molasses goodness coating his tongue and sliding down to create a celebration in his stomach.

Incredible.

He lifted the small piece left in his hand, peered at it, then looked closer at the trays around the room. He knew these cookies.

"I've had this before."

"I brought you a plate of them less than a week ago."

He shook his head. "I tossed those out."

"You threw out my cookies?" Outrage and shock rang out, her voice rising with each word. Eyes wide, mouth half-open, she kept trying to say something but the words seemed to be stuck somewhere. Instead she shook her head and gestured, tried again, then settled on a low growl.

Brody smothered a laugh.

Well, well.

He'd intimidated her.

He'd groped her.

He'd put on his meanest face and tried to scare her.
And she'd had a sassy comeback every single time.
But now he'd finally done it.
He'd rendered Genna Reilly speechless.
All it'd taken was to insult her cookies.
He couldn't help it. He laughed out loud.

Shock faded, leaving Genna's expression blank before it slowly shifted to fury. Red washed over her cheeks and her eyes sparked enough fire to turn the cookies to charcoal.

"I'm sorry?" he offered, trying to smother his laughter. It was hard, though. She was so damned cute with her outrage.

"For…?"

What? She wanted a detailed list? Oh, no. He might limit his experience with women to the length of a long weekend. But he wasn't stupid. The minute he started confessing, she'd start keeping score. Since she was ahead of the game anyway, he wasn't about to hand her that kind of ammo.

"You know," he said slowly, changing the subject. "Every month my gramma sent me a care package. Wherever I was, I'd get a box of cookies. Sugar cookies in Cairo, spice cookies in Dubai. In Korea I got a box of chocolate chunk that were so good, the entire SEAL team was licking crumbs out of the box."

"So?" Her expression didn't change. But the way her eyes lit with pleasure assured Brody he was right in his suspicions.

"So, for the last eight years, I've been getting cookies from my grandmother. Except they weren't from her."

"Did she say they were?" Genna asked, moving the cooled cookies to a rack before turning back to whatever other delicious concoction she was whipping up.

"Nope. Not once did she say, 'Brody, I made these cookies myself,'" he acknowledged. "But neither did she ever mention they were from someone else."

He waited a beat while Genna poured white batter into what looked like small pie tins.

"Any idea what's behind the covert cookie care package?" he asked as soon as she set the bowl down.

"Maybe you should ask her," Genna said, leaning forward so her hair swung down, hiding her face as she arranged the tins in a pan of shallow water.

"I'm asking you."

Genna slid the tray into the oven, then with a sigh deep enough to do interesting things to her apron ruffles, she faced him with a shrug. Her shoulders hunched and she dropped her chin to her chest.

"I made the cookies," she confessed with more guilt than most insurgents he'd watched be interrogated.

"No! Really?"

Some of the shame faded as her lips twitched. But the odd look didn't leave her eyes. Like she was hiding something still. Something ugly. What? Since he hadn't dropped dead, he knew she hadn't poisoned the cookies.

"Why?" he asked. When she pressed her lips together, he shook his head. "C'mon. Why would you send cookies all that time through my gramma? How'd you get her to go along with it? She's not known for keeping secrets, but she never hinted. Even when I thanked her to her face for the treats and told her how much the guys loved them."

"She told me that," Genna said softly. He assumed her affectionate smile was for his grandmother. Then, after giving him a long look and probably realizing he wasn't going to give it up, she lifted both hands in the air.

"Look, it's no big deal. I'd just moved in here and was going around meeting the neighbors. I took Irene cookies and when I realized how lonely she was, I started taking them by each week. She mentioned once that you'd loved cookies when you were a little boy. So I gave her extras. What she did with the extras was totally up to her."

There was more to it than that. But Genna had that stubborn tilt going with her chin, so he knew he wouldn't get the rest of the story. Yet.

Just as well.

The idea of her sending him cookies, of her thinking about him every single month for the last eight years. That did something to him. A warmth Brody had never felt spread through him, soft and gentle. Probably heartburn from eating so many sweets on an empty stomach, he told himself.

Still, better to drop the subject than risk feeding that feeling.

"So, seriously. What's with all the food? Is that what you do when you aren't playing messenger for the mayor? You have a bakery?"

"No. And I'm not the mayor's messenger. I'm the community liaison. I work with the various businesses and organizations on things like outreach, civic issues, beautification and events." She looked around the room and must have noticed there was three square inches of counter space available, so she pulled out a big bowl and started gathering ingredients.

"That's your real job? I thought it was something you did like volunteering. You know, being a good citizen and all." He grabbed a muffin, figuring if she was baking something else she could use the room.

"Why are you here again?" she asked, lifting her chin and giving him as cool look. "You just wanted to visit because my father put me on the off-limits list? Or did you get lonely there in that tiny house all by yourself with nobody to insult?"

Brody grinned. He loved her claws.

But she had a point.

And while he wasn't big on apologies, he did owe her something after the way he'd treated her before. He looked at the muffin in his hand and grimaced. He hated explaining himself. Especially when he didn't really understand why he was here. Just that he'd needed to see her.

"I didn't realize how hard things might be for you," he said slowly. When she frowned and shook her head in confusion, he clarified. "Here, after. I figured you'd skate through, you know? Pampered princess and all that."

She pulled a weird spoon thing made up of wires out of a drawer, running it through her hands as she considered his words.

"After? You mean when my father shanghaied you into the navy?"

Brody almost choked on his muffin laughing.

"Yeah. After that." Leave it to Genna to tell it like it was.

"I'm pretty sure you're the only person in the world who thinks I'm a pampered princess," she said, rolling her eyes and ignoring the rest of his words.

So. She didn't want to talk about what it'd been like.

Too bad. Brody did.

"What happened? I thought you were going to some fancy college. Didn't Joe say you'd gotten into Stanford?" Not that Joe bragged about his sister. If Brody remembered correctly, Joe'd been bitching that Genna's accomplishments were putting pressure on him. Apparently their parents were starting to nag that he get off his ass and do something with his life.

Genna pressed her lips together, all of her attention on the milky sugar mixture she was stirring with that weird spoon. After a few seconds, she shrugged.

"That didn't work out. I ended up staying here and did the community college thing instead."

Maybe it was because all he'd ever wanted to do was

get the hell out of Bedford, but Brody just wasn't buying that she'd given up so easily on leaving.

Or maybe it was the way she refused to look at him.

Deciding this was going to take a while and he might as well be comfortable, he pulled out one of the ladder-back chairs, turned it backward and straddled it.

"Comfy?" she asked, the sarcasm as thick as the cream she was stirring.

"I could use something to drink," Brody responded. "But otherwise, thanks, I'm pretty comfortable."

After a long look, she walked over to the sink, took a glass out of the cabinet and filled it with tap water. Since it gave Brody a great view of her butt, he couldn't complain. Except that he wasn't here to look at her butt, he reminded himself. He was here to find out what the hell had happened to her life after he'd left.

"You didn't get to go to Stanford because of what happened between us?" he guessed, watching her face closely. "Was that your punishment for getting too close to a bad influence?"

She sighed, looking defeated for the first time he'd ever seen. Her entire being, face, body and spirit, seemed to sag.

"Do you blame me for your impromptu commitment to the military?" she asked, sidestepping his question. Again.

"No." For a couple of years, he'd wanted to. But he'd never quite been able to justify it as fair.

"Then you shouldn't have any trouble understanding that I don't blame you for my parents going off the deep end with the overprotective control issues."

"What happened?" Brody was as surprised at his words as Genna seemed to be. He never asked questions like that. He always figured people overshared anyway, so why encourage more? But all of a sudden, with Genna, he wanted to know everything.

Maybe he was suffering delayed reactions from his injuries. Or was in desperate need of a distraction from the upcoming therapy and return to base. But he couldn't let it go. He had to know what had happened.

The buzzer chimed just then and she slid a thick mitten on her hand to pull out the little cake things she'd put in earlier. She touched the tops, added more water to the pan, then slid it all back in the oven and reset the timer. That should have given Brody plenty of time to talk himself out of the idiotic idea brewing in his head.

He didn't quite manage it, though.

"Maybe we could try something new," Brody said quietly.

Spooning the fluffy white cream she'd been stirring into a triangular shaped plastic bag, Genna glanced over. Heat flared in her eyes, making it clear she'd be interested in trying quite a few things. She wet her lips so they glistened, tempting him to ignore his conscience and give in to the need to taste her again. But instead of making any suggestions that could open the door to tasting, touching or anything else that'd feel great and show incredibly bad judgment, she arched one brow in inquiry.

"What'd you want to try?"

Brody tried the words out in his head, but they sounded too stupid to say aloud. Holy crap, he felt like a dorky schoolboy. Any second now he'd be shuffling his feet and, God forbid, blushing.

"Brody?"

He sighed, then faced the words the way he faced Hell Week, that sky full of empty air when he was jumping from a plane, and enemy fire. With a deep sigh, a straight spine and an unbreakable resolve.

"I thought we could try being friends."

9

FRIENDS.

She and Brody Lane were friends.

Or at least, they were trying to be.

She wasn't sure how she felt about it, though. She'd agreed because, well, she wanted to know the real Brody Lane. To find out if he was different from the guy she'd spent years fantasizing about.

Over the last couple weeks, she'd discovered three things.

He was completely different from the guy she'd thought he was. He was controlled and strong-willed, and didn't hesitate to voice his beliefs.

He was exactly the same as the guy she'd thought he was. Quiet, almost to the point of being taciturn, clever and fun when he did have something to say, and so sexy that she got turned on just watching him breathe.

And, over the last few days, she'd come to realize that they actually could be friends. That they had enough in common, similar interests and values. That they'd found a rhythm and flow that felt good. And as great as that was, she would absolutely, positively, unquestionably go crazy if all Brody would ever be was her friend.

Genna peered into the mirror, trying to see if there was crazy shining in her eyes yet. Nope. A few hints of stress and a whole lot of sexual frustration, but no signs of crazy.

Just her normal blue gaze stared back at her, albeit wearing a little more makeup than usual. Her eyes were smudged in kohl, with a dusky gray shadow giving her a smoky, do-me-all-night look she'd practiced for hours. Pale pink lips with a hint of shimmer on her cheekbones and she was as close to sophisticated sexy as she figured she'd ever get.

She leaned back from the mirror, lifting her hair this way and that. Up or down? Down said casual, just two friends going to dinner. If anyone saw her and Brody together, she could play it off as just a friendly meet-up with a distant acquaintance. Up said fancy, maybe a date. There was no way to pass off fancy hair as a casual get-together. Fancy hair said she'd put in time, effort. That she was looking to score.

Which she was.

But she didn't want anyone else knowing that.

Including Brody, who seemed completely determined to keep their relationship—or friendship, as he always corrected her—on his terms. Which included his stopping by at random times over the last week, eating cookies, testing her new recipes and nagging her to do something with her baking instead of giving it away. He didn't talk much, but listened just fine as long as the conversation wasn't about him. Which meant Genna did all the talking. She hadn't realized how much she had to say, things she couldn't say to the other people in her life. Frustrations and worries, dreams and fears.

But nothing about them. Nothing personal. The minute she'd bring up that night ten years ago, Brody would shut it down. If she mentioned their first meeting two weeks ago, he changed the subject.

And the few times she'd tried flirting?

He'd walked out.

Genna dropped her hair and pressed her fingers to her temples.

Clearly, it was going to be a hair-down kind of evening.

But she wanted it up.

She sighed. Yeah. She was going crazy.

"Hey."

Genna jumped.

She'd been so focused on her image, she hadn't heard Macy come in.

Her stomach tightened with nerves that had nothing to do with Brody, but everything to do with her relationship with him.

"What're you doing here?" she asked, glancing from Macy to the clock. Brody wasn't due for twenty minutes. Hopefully she could shoo her friend out before he got here.

"I came by to borrow your printer. The caterer emailed me the final contract," Macy said, her tone distracted as she gave Genna a suspicious twice-over. Clearly the first glance had tipped her off. Genna brushed her fingers over her hair, hanging loose and casual, and bit her lip.

"What're you doing?" Macy asked, stepping farther into the room. Her gaze swept from Genna's dress to the three others tossed on the bed, then landed on the tangled pile of shoes next to the closet. Her arched brows demanded information.

Genna didn't want to give it to her, though.

Macy would judge. And since Brody had been stubbornly reluctant to take his hero dues, especially in public, the gossip had shifted. Now the lunchtime buzz wasn't as much about Brody Lane, the military hero. It was more speculation with a whole lot of rehashing his past.

Macy, like Genna's parents, would buy into the speculation, rather than trusting the hero buzz.

"I'm just trying on outfits. You know, playing girl for a change." Just because she lived most of her life in jeans didn't mean she didn't have a great wardrobe of things she never got to wear anywhere. Especially the shoes. A girl who stood five-ten barefoot and only seemed to date insecure men never got to wear heels. Since Brody was secure as hell and six-two, she'd figured this was a great time to scuff those soles.

But she didn't want to tell Macy that, either.

"You're going out?"

"Maybe."

"With Stewart?" Macy said, looking at the four-inch, pointed-toe stiletto pumps on Genna's feet.

"Eww. No. He collects troll dolls. Remember?"

"Then who are you going out with?"

Crap. Genna gave the clock a wincing glance and realized she wasn't going to get out of this. She took a deep breath and put on her most confident face.

"With a friend for a friendly dinner. Sort of repayment for a few dozen cookies, a cake and a couple of pies. You know how everyone pays me for my baked goods in favors or in exchange?"

"I don't remember you getting all dressed up when Mr. Jenson bought you lunch last month for making his granddaughter birthday cupcakes."

"That's because Mr. Jenson bought me a hoagie and a side of fruitcake off the lunch truck and he didn't even invite me to the party." And, of course, there was the fact that the sixty-year-old pharmacist looked nothing like her hot and hunky SEAL.

"So. Who's been eating your cookies?" Macy asked suspiciously.

Sadly, no one. Since Macy wouldn't understand or appreciate that joke, Genna just shrugged.

"Genna…"

"Brody Lane," she blurted out, throwing her hands in the air. "There. Now you know. I'm going to dinner—a casual, just-between-friends dinner—with Brody Lane."

From the horror in her eyes and the drop of Macy's chin, maybe it'd have been better if she'd said she was going to dinner with an ax murderer.

"Like I said, it's just a thank-you meal. No big deal."

Macy's mouth worked, but nothing came out. Good. Genna knew she wasn't going to like hearing it when her friend recovered.

Pretending her spine wasn't so tight it'd take a chiropractor and a sledgehammer to crack it, she moved to the full-length mirror to check her dress. Was it too fancy for a simple dinner between friends?

Red and fitted with a sweetheart neckline that made the most of the very little she had, the bodice hugged her body to the waist before flaring into full pleats to just above her knees.

She sneaked a glance at Macy's expression in the mirror. The other woman looked like she figured a straitjacket would be a better fit.

"Okay. What? Go ahead and say whatever you have to say. But do it fast, because Brody's going to be here in ten minutes and I'm leaving."

"You're crazy. Don't you remember what happened last time you chased after this guy? How furious your parents were? In case you forgot, your mom ended up in the hospital and your brother in jail."

Praying for patience, Genna reminded herself that this was her oldest, dearest friend. And that she was too heavy to throw out the window.

"Joe stole a car. That had nothing to do with me, my actions or Brody. He would have gone to jail even if I was sitting at home eating popcorn and watching reruns of *Friends*." Something she'd told herself, and her parents, a million times over. Dammit, she wasn't to blame for her brother's choices. "And Mom went to the hospital because she had an asthma attack. Again, in no way related to my actions that night."

"Her asthma attack could have been brought on by stress," Macy said, parroting Cara so perfectly that it was all Genna could do to not look around the room for her mother.

Or cry.

"That doesn't mean I caused the stress. Joe gets the lion's share of the credit for that. Or it could have been brought on by the heat." Genna frowned, wondering why the hell she was always to blame for everything when she was the least of the contributors. When did she get to stop paying for her brother's choices? And when the hell would someone trust her to run her own life?

Trying for patience, she smiled through gritted teeth. "Macy, my mom is a hypochondriac. Even the doctor says so. My brother was on a collision course with himself."

And Genna had paid, and paid and paid and paid, for that night. As horrible as she felt about Joe's choices, about what'd finally happened to him, she was tired of paying.

"It's no big deal. Seriously, don't get all weirded out." Genna wanted to check her lipstick, but figured primping would negate her entire pitch. "Brody is staying at his gramma's while he recovers, so he's living across the alley and we've run into each other a few times. Partially because the mayor wants to do an event for him. Hero's welcome and all that."

Something Brody had no interest in. Still, Genna had started putting together tentative ideas, in case she changed his mind. After all, he was a hero and maybe if he saw how much the town appreciated his service, he'd have a different opinion of Bedford. And of the idea of visiting here more often after he'd gone back on duty.

And maybe after seeing Brody praised and paraded, everyone would see what a great guy he was. A much better guy than someone like, oh, say Stewart.

"It's really no big deal," she said again. This time as much to convince herself as Macy.

"You're going on a date. For Valentine's Day."

"We're going to dinner. On a Tuesday," Genna corrected, checking her purse for necessities. "Valentine's isn't until Friday."

Lipstick, keys, license and credit card, condom, twenty-dollar bill, cell phone.

Looked as if she was all set.

"Hey, there's nothing between us. We're friends. That's it. That's all he wants." She met Macy's eyes and straight up lied. "And that's all I want."

"Fine." Macy huffed, then handed Genna the black leather gloves and wool jacket from the chair, as if covering her as much as possible before she went downstairs was going to keep her virtue intact. "When's he leaving?"

Leaving? The thought was like a jagged knife ripping through her gut. She hated thinking about life without Brody.

"He's going to Coronado four times a week for physical therapy now, so I'd imagine he'll be back to full use of his leg before the end of the month." She gave Macy a big smile all the brighter for being fake. "So he should be back on duty in two weeks."

A smart girl would start steeling her heart against the end. A smarter girl would cut things off now, before her emotions got tangled any tighter.

Genna was smart.

Damned smart.

Smart enough to know that she was already in too deep. She had been for years. She was smart enough to know that nothing was going to make the heartbreak of Brody leaving any easier to take. So she was going to get every second of pleasure, of fun and of anything else she could from these couple of weeks together.

And she didn't care if it took her thirteen of her fourteen days. At some point before he left to play hero again, she was getting him naked and naughty.

Right on cue, the doorbell rang.

"Don't you have something to print?" she asked, hurrying around her friend and heading for the stairs. "Go ahead, take your time. Lock up when you leave."

Never one to take a hint, Macy followed her right down the stairs and stood there like a grumpy rain cloud, waiting for Genna to open the door.

Trying to ignore her, Genna tossed her coat over the hall bench, took a deep breath, put on a big smile and opened the door.

And almost melted as the chilly evening air washed over her. Oh, he looked good. Black slacks and dress shirt suited his bad-boy image and fit to perfection. So used to seeing him in jeans or sweats and a tee, she had to swallow a couple of times to keep from drooling.

"Hi," she finally said.

"Hey. You look nice." His tone was light and friendly, but his eyes were hot as they swept over her body, leaving the kind of tingles that led to tight nipples, damp panties and, hopefully, multiple orgasms.

Yes. Genna wanted to do a happy dance right there in the doorway. Finally, he was looking at her as something other than a friendly cookie machine.

Maybe they could skip dinner and get right to dessert.

The loud cough behind her burst the sexual bubble as effectively as an icy cold blast from the hose.

Brody looked over her shoulder. She followed his gaze and sighed.

"Brody, this is my friend Macy. She was just leaving," Genna said pointedly.

"Hi," Brody offered with a polite nod.

Looking distant, as if she were holding her breath in case he was carrying a bad case of cooties, Macy gave a jerky nod.

Brody glanced at Genna, who just rolled her eyes and gestured him inside.

"You look great," she said as the door closed behind him. Her fingers itched to straighten his collar, to feel the fabric of his shirt and see if it was as soft as it looked. "I didn't realize you had fancy clothes with you."

"I stopped by barracks after physical therapy today."

Brody shifted from foot to foot, almost as if he'd rather be in front of a firing squad. Whether that preference was over what he was wearing, his visit to his barracks or this evening's plans was up in the air.

"You sure you want to go into San Diego? We can eat someplace here in town instead. That way you don't have to drive," he said, referring to the fact that while he'd come back on his Harley after his last physical therapy session, he didn't have a car.

Nope. Dinner in San Diego was more romantic. A drive would give them time to talk. And if they stayed here, people would see. Then they'd talk. Her father would hear and things would get ugly. Worse, her mother would hear and head straight for the hospital.

"Good question. You should eat in town. I hear Ziapatta's is serving lasagna tonight," Macy broke in. Stepping forward, she started reciting the menu as if her life—or Genna's virtue—depended on convincing Brody to eat there.

Genna scowled. The woman couldn't say hello, but she saw a chance to ruin the night and she turned into a chatterbox.

"We have reservations," Genna interrupted smoothly. "And I don't want Italian food."

She wanted her date, dammit.

"Good night, Macy," she said emphatically.

As huffs went, Macy was a champion. Muttering warnings the whole way, she skirted around them to yank open the front door, then stormed down the walk.

Genna grimaced at the scowl her friend threw over her shoulder before climbing into her car.

"I'll bet she's on the phone by the end of the street," she predicted, letting the door slam shut with a satisfying bang.

"Gossip?" Brody guessed.

"Tattling."

He glanced out the window at the departing car, then arched a brow her way.

"To whom about what?"

"To my parents about us," Genna said, heading over to grab her purse and coat off the bench.

She didn't make it far.

Two steps and she was stopped by Brody's hand on her arm.

"Hold up a sec. So let me get this straight. Your friend is going to run to your mommy and daddy and stir up trouble when she tells them that you're hanging out with me?"

Genna frowned for a second at his use of hanging out instead of dating. He was working hard to keep that wall between them. Or maybe it wasn't hard work on his part and he really did only think of her as someone to hang out with while he was stuck in town.

Then, taking a deep breath to shake that off because she was sure she'd change his mind eventually, she focused on his question. And the irritation on his face.

"Totally obnoxious, right? I know she's my best friend, and she really is a sweetie. But she's always doing stuff like this. She thinks she knows best, and just has to interfere."

Genna started to move toward the bench and her coat again, but Brody didn't let go of her arm.

"What?" she asked.

His irritation had settled into a scowl.

"Tell me something. Other than your friend, does anyone know you're hanging out with me?"

Again with the hanging out? Genna huffed, then shrugged. He let go this time, but shifted so his arms were crossed and his legs wide. She had the feeling that even if she did get her coat, she wasn't getting past him to open the front door.

"I don't know," she said, throwing both her hands in the air. "I suppose your gramma knows. And people have seen us together, right?"

At her corner grocery store. The little café on the edge of town. The movie theater matinee. Nobody who knew and might report back to her parents. But that was beside the point. They were still people.

"You ashamed?"

He said it so matter-of-factly, with no inflection at all, that it took a few seconds for the implication of his words to sink in.

"Of course I'm not ashamed to be *hanging out* with you," she protested, ignoring the guilty little tickle in the back of her throat at the words.

He didn't look convinced. In fact, if Genna didn't know better, she'd think he was a little hurt. But Brody didn't care about things like approval. And, despite the fact that they were playing this *let's be friends* game of his, she doubted her opinion registered in his world.

"Yeah? But you're worried about your friend ratting you out. Worried enough about word getting around that you only wanna be seen with me if we're out of town." Brody pulled a contemplative face and rocked back on his heels, then gave a decisive nod. "Yep. You're ashamed."

Genna's jaw dropped in a shocked gasp. She took a step backward, but figured pressing one hand to her heart might be overkill. He wasn't buying it anyway. Brody was still giving her that pitying look, as if she'd just admitted to sleeping with his photo cut from a high school yearbook under her pillow. Which she hadn't done for at least nine years.

"Oh, and you're one to talk," she tossed back. "If it hadn't been for my father warning you to stay away from me, you'd never have come over."

He just stared, no expression in those gold eyes. Damn that SEAL training of his. So Genna pushed harder.

"What's the difference? Isn't you being with me your own form of rebellion? A way to give the finger to the guy who shipped you off ten years ago?"

Well, that changed his expression. Right from casual suspicion to icy distance.

Oops. Maybe she'd pushed a little too far.

"I'm your rebellion?"

Genna winced. Leave it to him to home in on that one particular statement. Couldn't he focus on the insult instead? It'd be a lot easier to smooth that over.

"Aren't we going to dinner?" she asked in her brightest, let's-change-the-subject tone. "We're going to be late if we don't get on the road, and I'm starving already."

His expression didn't shift.

"I don't think you're doing it right," he mused, his slow contemplative tone at odds with the cold look in his eyes. "If you want to rebel, you throw your actions in people's faces. You don't hide your bad side away hoping nobody will notice."

You did if you were afraid of their reaction. Genna pressed her lips together to keep that confession to herself.

"Then, by your own definition, I'm not rebelling," she pointed out with a teasing smile, hoping to charm him out of pursuing this conversation. "And we've already established that I'm not ashamed of being seen with you. So why are we wasting time talking about this? Especially since chitchat is right up there with wearing pink on your list of manly things to do."

"Because I don't like being played."

This was getting ridiculous. Genna took a couple of deep breaths, trying to push away the edges of panic that were pressing down on her. She was so close to her dream. So close to having something—maybe not a relationship, but something—with Brody. And now it was shattering so fast she couldn't even see where the pieces were flying.

"I'm not playing you. I'm not ashamed of you." She shifted, lifting her chin and giving him a direct look filled with all the sincerity she had. "And I'm not using you to rebel."

"Right."

There was so much sarcasm in that single word that Genna was tempted to look at the floor to see if it was dripping on her feet. What was his problem?

"Don't you think you're blowing this out of proportion? I just said that Macy was a tattletale."

"Exactly. C'mon, Genna," he said, shaking his head. "You're all grown up and still living under your parents' thumbs. What better way to wiggle out than to piss them off by dating the guy they blame for introducing their princess to the dark side?"

"Why are you doing this?" she asked quietly. "Are you trying to pick a fight? If you didn't want to go to dinner, all you had to do was say so. Friends don't hurt friends, Brody."

DIRECT HIT.

Brody grimaced at the baffled pain in Genna's eyes. Why was he doing this?

He shoved his hands into the pockets of his slacks to keep his fists from finding a wall to pound on. He had so much anger broiling inside him, but it wasn't aimed at her.

He didn't give a damn if she was rebelling. Hell, she deserved to. Her parents were manipulative assbites who were ruining her life with their fears.

It made no difference to him if she hid their relationship, either. She was the one who was going to have to live with the talk after he was gone, not him.

As she said. Friends didn't hurt friends.

But Brody was a lousy friend. Just ask Carter.

"I should go," he decided.

"No," she said quickly. "What is going on? I thought we were going to dinner. I thought we were friends. So either feed me or talk to me, but you aren't leaving until you do one or the other."

She was so damned cute when she got feisty. Brody couldn't help but smile a little. Actually, she was so damned cute all the time, feisty or not. And sexy. Fascinating, entertaining, fun.

His smile fell away.

Maybe that was part of the problem.

He'd thought they could be friends. He hadn't been able to resist spending time with her, and had thought he could control the intense attraction he felt for her. That he could channel it into making up for some of the lousy deal she'd gotten after he'd left.

But he felt as if he'd signed up for a torture project. Days spent talking and joking. Watching her bake, listening to her dreams. Nights spent hard and horny, diving into dreams so hot he thought the bed was on fire. He was a man used to pushing through the pain, well trained to overcome his body's weaknesses. Except, apparently, the ones Genna inspired.

"Look," he said, taking a deep breath and hoping for

some semblance of tact and diplomacy. "This friendship thing, it was a mistake."

Her eyes widened, surprise and hurt flashing. Then, with a sweep of her lashes, her expression changed. Intensified. It sent an itch down Brody's spine.

"We're not going to be friends anymore?" she asked in a calm, friendly tone. If it wasn't for the fact that she was saying the right words, he'd have figured she hadn't understood him.

As soon as he nodded, she gave him a brilliant smile and tossed off her coat. It hit the floor with a swoosh just as she reached behind her back. The move was quickly accompanied by the sound of a zipper. And Brody's hiss.

"What, exactly, do you think you're doing?" he asked, hoping like hell it wasn't what he thought she was doing.

"Seducing you."

Damn.

That's what he'd been afraid of.

Brody's breath was a little labored, but he tried to reel in his reaction. This wasn't happening, he warned his dick. No point getting ready for a party they weren't gonna attend.

His dick, always ready to party, ignored him and hardened rock-solid anyway.

"Genna—" he started to say.

But she interrupted before he could figure out the rest of his protest.

"I figure this is part one of a two-part solution to our problem," she said. "You were trying to pretend we're just friends. Except we aren't. We might be building a friendship. But what we are is crazy attracted to each other. So part one is to act on that attraction once and for all. The total act, with you naked. I'm willing to be on top if you're still holding on to that friendship myth of yours. That way you can tell yourself I took advantage."

Brody couldn't help but laugh. Sure, the sound was strangled and a little painful. But it was the best he could do with the blood streaming south so fast his head was spinning.

She tugged at one sleeve, the red fabric tight from wrist to shoulder. Then she tugged at the other to loosen it, too.

"And then there's the issue of you thinking I'm ashamed of you. I figure after we've had our way with each other's bodies a few times, we're going to be hungry. We can go to the nearby café and get something to eat. Since I figure you're really good at sex, even if I am on top, what we'll have been doing will be obvious. That should take care of that issue."

He made some sort of choking sound, sure if he had any blood left in his brain it would have been words of protest.

Then she let her dress fall to the floor. Brody actually gulped trying not to swallow his tongue.

She was gorgeous.

Ivory limbs glowed like silk, the long sleek length of her interrupted by tiny pieces of black lace. He didn't know where to start. At the top, where the lace cupped the gentle slope of her breasts. Or at the bottom, where it was barely held in place by two tiny strings.

His gaze as hot as the blood rushing through his body, he decided to settle for the middle. At the cherry-red jewel decorating her belly button.

Screw friendship. And screw good sense.

He was gonna let Genna Reilly seduce him.

10

GENNA HADN'T HAD many opportunities to be ballsy and brave in her life. So she figured she'd been saving up, and this was the perfect time to put every bold instinct she possessed to work.

She didn't want Brody's thinking she was ashamed of him standing in the way of whatever they were building together. If it took being outed to her parents to prove that, then fine.

She wanted Brody Lane.

And, dammit, after ten years, she was finally going to have him.

Except he was standing there, fully clothed and still wearing his coat, one hand flexed as if reaching for the doorknob.

And she was standing here, almost naked except her undies and high heels. It wasn't that she minded the almost-naked part. It was the clothing inequality that bothered her. And the fact that he wasn't making any moves to change it.

Her bravado waned a smidge. What had she been thinking? That he'd take one look at her underwear, lose his mind and do her against the wall? Clearly her thinking needed an adjustment. Since her state of nakedness did, too, her fingers itched to grab her dress.

Then she saw the look in his eyes. It was as if the golden depths had turned molten, his gaze was so hot. She saw his jaw clench, and the pulse at the base of his throat was pounding hard.

Relief surging through her, washing away the nerves and making way for desire, Genna almost did a happy dance right there in the entryway.

He wanted her. Maybe not enough to grab her and do her against the wall, but that look made her think that maybe she could change his mind.

Knowing that, she didn't feel naked anymore.

She felt powerful.

"C'mon, big boy," she said, her tone husky and suggestive. "Let's see what you've got."

Brody laughed, just as she'd hoped he would. Then, his eyes still hot and locked on her body, he shrugged off his jacket and stepped closer. Close enough to touch.

She didn't wait for him to make the first move.

She'd said she was seducing him, and she meant it.

So she grabbed hold of his shirt and pulled him closer, ignoring the ping as one of his buttons flew off and hit the wall. In heels, she was tall enough that all she had to do was tilt her head back to meet his mouth. So tilt she did, one hand wrapping around the back of his neck and holding tight.

As his mouth took hers, she was grateful she was holding on. Oh, my. Her mind spun in a slow, delicious circle.

It was like he was starving and she a feast.

His tongue swept in, plunging deep. Demanding a response that was hard to offer while her body was melting into a puddle of lust.

But Genna did her best. Her tongue danced with his, their lips sliding in hot need against each other. The moves rolled, one into another, and she could barely think as the passion pounded through her veins.

His hands swept along her arms so light and soft they were barely there, leaving tingles of needy heat. He reached her wrists and bracketed each loosely between his fingers.

Then, so fast she didn't even realize what was happening, he had her up against the wall.

Genna almost came right then and there. Her core throbbed, wet and hot. Her thighs trembled and her mind went completely blank. All she could do was feel. And she felt incredible.

Trapped between the cool plaster and his hard, hot body, she wrapped one leg around his thigh to pull him closer. He gripped her hands, both of them, and lifted them above her head, anchoring them there with one of his while he slid the other into her hair to lift her face closer.

His kiss was voracious.

His teeth scraped her lower lip, tugging it into his mouth, then sucking. Genna whimpered. His tongue swept over the tender flesh as if soothing it, then plunged into her mouth again.

His fingers skimmed along the back of her neck, tugging at her hair to hold her mouth in place, totally at his mercy. A part of her reveled in the power he had over her. That he demanded.

Another part, though, wanted to make demands of her own. She wanted to touch him. To run her hands over those muscles and feel how hard they could get. To measure the tantalizing width of his shoulders, the rigid length of his thighs. And all the other hard, wide and long things he might be willing to share.

She shifted to release her hands from his grip. But he wouldn't let go.

A thrill surged through her system, from the tips of her

fingers to the aching bud between her thighs. She tugged harder, but his grip didn't change. He was in control.

Or so he thought.

Unable to use her hands, Genna slid her foot down the back of his thigh to his calf, using the move to press her core tighter against his hip. Then she slid her foot back up, gripping him tight.

He growled, low and sexy in his throat.

She arched her back to press her breasts against his chest. The move made her nipples tighten to rigid buds, aching for attention.

As if he'd heard their plea, he skimmed his hand down the side of her throat and slid it between their bodies to cup her breast. She swelled, aching and needy, against the lace of her bra trying to get closer to the hard warmth of his palm.

Her breath came faster now. Her pulse raced and her heart pounded so hard, she was sure he could feel it.

"More," she breathed against his lips.

"How much more?" His fingers dipped between the edge of her bra and her skin, rubbing his knuckles back and forth along her nipple. She squirmed, pressing herself tighter against his thigh, desperate to ease the mounting pressure there.

"Everything you've got," she gasped.

He leaned back. She gave a shuddering sigh, her arms moving to reach for him. But although he lowered his hand so her arms were bent above her head, he didn't let go.

Instead, he used his free hand to pull the lace cup of her bra down so it lifted her breast. For a long, exhilarating moment he stared. His eyes were hot, intense. His breath short and the look on his face as needy as the desire contracting low in Genna's belly.

He brushed one finger, just the tip, over her nipple.

Genna whimpered.

He leaned forward, this time touching his tongue to her pebbled peak. He pulled back just a little and blew.

Genna's thighs quivered, her clitoris trembling. She pressed harder against his thigh, undulating, desperate to relieve the pressure.

His free hand skimmed over her stomach, fingers leaving a hot trail all the way to the slender elastic band of her thong. He traced the lace from front to back, then reached out to cup his large hand over her butt, squeezing her cheek and pulling her tight against him. Angling her perfectly.

Oh, God.

Her body started shaking.

He bent his head, taking her nipple into his mouth. Sucking hard. Swirling his tongue around, nipping, then swirling again. His hand slid beneath her thigh, his fingers touching the wet bud there. He gently pinched her clitoris, making her cry out.

So close.

Her body was so tight.

The orgasm right there, just out of reach.

Now.

She needed it now.

He didn't bother pushing her panties aside. Instead, with a quick snap of his fingers, he ripped the lace so the fabric fell to the floor between their feet.

Sucking hard on her nipple, it wasn't until he pinched the other one that she realized he'd let go of her arms.

Unable to remember what she'd wanted to do with her hands, unable to do anything else, she gripped his shoulders so tight her nails dug into his flesh.

He slid two fingers along the length of her swollen clit. Up, then down, then up again.

The climax coiled tighter.

Then he thrust one finger inside her, swirling while his thumb worked her bud.

The climax snapped.

Genna's head flew back against the wall, her eyes closed tight as stars exploded in time with the orgasm pounding through her.

He didn't stop sucking or thrusting.

She didn't stop coming.

Not until everything went black, the stars behind her eyes fading. The orgasm was still coming in tiny shudders now, her slick flesh still vibrating around his finger.

Her breath tore from a throat so dry, she had to try three times just to swallow.

He shifted, leaving a chill where his body had been.

"Where are you going?" she cried, not done with him yet.

"I want to taste you."

Ohhhh. The walls of her insides quivered again, a tiny orgasm exploding at his words.

But as much as she wanted to score as many climaxes as she could, she wanted something else more.

She wanted to touch him.

To see him.

For more than ten years, she'd dreamed of seeing him naked. Fantasized about what his body looked like. She wanted—no, needed—to see it. Now.

She grabbed his shirt, still loose around his shoulders.

"Not yet," she said, shaking her head.

His eyes met hers. The golden depths were molten with desire, narrowed in question.

"Strip first," she told him. "It's only fair."

His lips quirked to one side and he gave her body a considering look. Genna followed his gaze, realizing he'd pushed her bra beneath both of her breasts, the black lace vivid against her pale white flesh and berry-red nipples. Her panties were shredded, leaving the only other thing on her body a belly-button ring and a pair of black heels.

"I can strip later," he said, his words husky as he reached out one finger and slid it between her legs before lifting the wet proof of his handiwork to his lips. "I'm hungry now."

Genna's knees almost gave out. She had to take a couple of deep breaths to clear the haze from her eyes, then she forced herself to shake her head.

"Strip," she repeated, pushing the fabric of his shirt off his shoulders. And oh, baby, what shoulders they were. Pure muscle beneath silken flesh. Leaving him to deal with the buttons at his cuffs, she smoothed her hands over those shoulders. He was so warm, so hard.

She shifted forward, her lips brushing against that flesh.

She breathed in deeply, inhaling his scent, filling herself with his essence. Forgetting her orders, forgetting everything but exploring his chest with her mouth, she kissed her way over the delicious range of muscles, pausing to flick her tongue over one nipple before continuing her exploration.

She heard a thud, followed by another. But it was the weight of his slacks and belt hitting her toes that got her attention. Because that meant he'd gotten down to the good stuff. The stuff she wanted to play with most.

Unable to resist one last kiss, she then leaned back to check him out.

And almost came again, right then and there.

"Oh. My."

It was like she'd died and gone to heaven.

He was even bigger than she'd dreamed.

Her eyes locked on his penis as he stepped out of his pants, his toes pushing his socks off one foot, then the other. The move made that very, very large erection bounce.

Before she could look her fill, he dropped to his knees.

"What are you doing?" she objected.

"I stripped."

With no further explanation, his hands cupped her butt cheeks and pulled her closer. His tongue pressed between her damp curls, flicking and sucking.

Genna felt herself drowning again as desire washed over her.

"No," she gasped desperately. "Not yet."

His tongue paused. She moved fast, before he could overrule her. Or put that tongue back to work. One more lick and she was going to explode.

She fell to her knees, pressing him backward so fast he was too surprised to protest. As soon as he was on his back, she leaned down and took him into her mouth.

"Hey, now," he growled.

Still bent low, her hair trailing along his thighs, she shot him a mischievous smile.

"But I'm hungry, too."

He arched one brow, then shifted. Grabbing her by the hips, he lifted and turned her as if she weighed nothing. Now her knees straddled his chest and she was flashing him everything else. Before she could be embarrassed or self-conscious, actually before she could even blink, his tongue was back at work.

What's a girl to do, she thought, letting the sensations take over and bending low to slide her lips over the long, hard length of his arousal. Her head moved up and down, her mouth sucking and tongue swirling in time with his. His fingers gripped her thighs. Hers were braced flat on the floor. He pulled back just a little, blowing cool air over her wet flesh.

Genna's breath was coming in whimpering gasps now. She was so close, her body tight, the climax coiled low and intense. She lifted her head so her tongue danced around the velvet tip of his penis, then she sucked it into her mouth like a lollipop.

He growled.

His fingers gripped tighter and his mouth stilled for a moment, as if he were focusing on keeping control. Then, with a breath that gusted over her thighs, he sucked her clitoris into his mouth one more time, then thrust his tongue deep into her throbbing passage.

With a cry of shock, Genna exploded.

Her entire body shook with the power of her orgasm. She rode the waves, panting and oblivious to everything except the sensations, bigger, stronger than anything she'd ever felt in her life. More intense than anything she'd even fantasized about.

She didn't know how long it lasted. She didn't even realize that Brody had moved until she finally floated back to earth and realized she was lying on the floor now, wrapped in Brody's arms.

"Bed?"

"Here," she demanded, still panting from the power of her climax. She felt as if she'd climbed a very tall, very hard mountain. But she still had one more peak to scale. She slid her hand up and down the rock-hard velvet of his erection, then knowing how fast she could get distracted if she started touching him again, she quickly shifted away, grabbing her purse off the floor.

She didn't have a clue how he was going to top that incredible orgasm. Or even if he could.

But oh, baby, she was more than willing to let him try.

BRODY GROANED, NOT sure what he missed more. The warmth of her slender body against his. Or the feel of her talented fingers working their magic. He started to grab her back, then realized she was already on there, a condom held between two fingers like a trophy.

It was as if she'd read his mind. His grin was fast and just a little tight as need pounded through his system.

He reached for the foil wrapper. Quick as a cat, she

pulled it away. Wiggling her brows, she tore it open herself, the move slow and deliberate. After a quick glance for placement, she locked her eyes on his, forcing him to meet her wicked gaze as she slid the latex over his throbbing cock.

The effect of her eyes watching his reaction, and the way she slid her fingers around the base of his dick, made him groan.

"Now," he growled, reaching for her. It had to be now. He'd never wanted anyone, anything, as much as he wanted her right this second. He was terrified he might even need her. But since most of the blood in his body was currently partying down south, his brain couldn't muster enough energy to worry about that.

He'd have plenty of time to worry later.

Now, he had to have her.

Since relinquishing control wasn't something he did long or well, he jackknifed into a sitting position, taking her mouth. Her eyes widened with surprise, then blurred with passion. He grabbed her waist and shifted their positions so she was beneath him. Her fingers clutching his shoulders, she wrapped her legs around his hips.

Mouths still locked together, he slid into her in a single smooth move that felt more natural than breathing. Buried deep, Brody had only a second to wonder at the sense of coming home before his body demanded more.

Eager to get past the strange emotions buffeting him, he slowly pulled away, sliding almost out. Then he plunged.

Pulling her mouth free of his, Genna gasped.

He plunged again. And again.

He arched his back, shifting higher on his knees so her hips were off the floor. Her feet anchored to the small of his back, she met his every thrust with a panting moan and a tiny undulating move of her own.

Those tiny moves were killing his control.

Brody's breath came faster.

His body tightened.

He thrust faster. Harder. Deeper.

More.

He had to have more of her.

He wanted all of her.

Genna's moans turned to whimpers, higher and higher. Her thighs locked tight around hips, her fingers trembling as she dug her nails into his biceps.

He slid back out, leaving just the tip of his dick in her warmth. Her eyes flew open and she gave him an urgent look.

Staring into those blue depths, Brody plunged again, burying himself as deep as he could get.

And watched her explode.

Her cry echoing in his head, her climax pulsating and clenching his cock, Brody followed her right over the edge. The orgasm was so seriously mind-blowing, he didn't know when he'd be able to think again. Instead, he collapsed against her, twisting just before they came together so they were on their sides.

And he held tight.

Genna's body felt like it'd been used, and used well.

She throbbed in places she'd never been aware she had.

Her skin tingled.

Her lips were too swollen to talk.

Her muscles too lax to move.

Thankfully, Brody had still been sporting the manly mojo. Somewhere between minutes and hours after they'd guaranteed she'd get turned on every time she walked through her front door, he'd swept her into his arms and carried her up the stairs.

When they'd fallen into bed together, she'd thought they'd sleep. She'd been almost there when he'd started

the whole amazing experience over again. He'd claimed
he wanted to see how it compared on a mattress.

Snuggled close, her face buried in the crook of his
shoulder and his arms tight around her, Genna had to say
it had compared pretty darned well.

"I'm thinking you had a lot more fun this evening than
if we'd gone to dinner," she said quietly, her tone teasing
as she swirled her fingers through the light dusting of hair
on his chest.

"I'm sorry about that," he murmured against her hair.

"I'm not," she said with a little laugh. "This was much,
much better."

"I had to go by barracks today to get something to
wear," he finally said, sounding as though he'd just confessed to wearing her undies. Maybe someone had given
him a bad time about dressing up for a date?

Still floating on a cloud of sexual delight, Genna sighed
at the memory of how hot he'd looked all dressed up. "And
I tore your buttons off. I'll sew them back so you don't
have to go get another shirt."

It was sweet, though, that he'd thought a dinner that
was just two friends hanging out necessitated a trip home
to get special clothes.

"I haven't been back since the accident. Since before we
shipped off on that last mission." Brody's words were quiet,
just a hint above a whisper. But Genna's heart clenched
at the pain in them. Her smile fell away, her breath knot-
ting in her throat. She wanted to shift up onto her elbow
so she could see his face in the moonlight, to try to figure
out why he was hurting so badly. But knowing he'd hate
that, she kept her head on his shoulder instead. And waited.

"We lost a guy on that mission. Seeing his empty bunk
was a reminder, you know?"

It was only a few words. But there was so much pain
in them, Genna could barely control her sob. She swal-

lowed hard, blinking to clear the burning from her eyes
and trying to get control. She knew the only thing Brody
would hate more than sharing his emotions was her dumping hers all over him.

"I wanted to let you know," he said, his words a whisper in the night. "You asked why I was such an ass when
I got here. It wasn't you. It was that."

Her teeth clenched tight to keep the hot torrent of tears
from falling, Genna had to take a couple of breaths through
her nose before she could find enough control to respond.

"Hey, now," she finally said softly, proud that her laugh
was only a little shaky. "I never called you an ass."

"I was acting like one."

"I'm not denying that," she said, finally in control
enough of her expression to shift to her elbow and look at
him. "I'm just saying that I didn't call you that."

His smile was more a twitch than a grin, but she'd take
what she could get. The moonlight softened his features,
casting a warm glow over the bed. It didn't blunt the impact of his vivid eyes, though. Genna was pretty sure nothing could.

"So that means you're not going to hold a grudge over
dinner?" he teased.

"Well…"

"I knew it." This time his smile was real.

"You can make it up to me, though."

"Yeah?" he asked, his eyes blurring with desire and
one hand cupping her breast. "Did you have something
in mind?"

"Actually, I was hoping we could try it with me on
top this time," she said, wriggling her brows suggestively.
"Now that I've had my way with you, it's your turn. Show
me what you've got, big boy."

That made him laugh. And thankfully, to lean down

to kiss her. Genna was grateful. She needed something to distract her from the tight ache in her heart.

The first two times, their lovemaking had been a wild ride, fast and furious with shades of desperation.

This time, Brody was calling the shots.

His moves were smooth, gentle. Pure confidence and delicious control. His lips never left hers as he shifted their positions so she was flat on her back. Fingers entwined, he trailed kisses over her cheek, along her jaw and down her throat.

Genna moaned when he reached that spot at the base of her neck, right where it met her collarbone. Desire coiled again, low in her belly. But this time it was mixed with a tenderness, a gentle sort of emotion she wasn't sure what to do with.

So she ignored it and focused on the rising passion.

His hand swept down her side, cupping her waist before sliding down to her thigh. Fingers gentle, he trailed his hand along her leg in a teasing move until he'd reached her aching core. Soft as a whisper, he worked her until she begged.

Then, finally, he shifted, looming large and hard over her before he slid, smooth as silk, into her welcoming warmth.

The minute he plunged, she exploded.

It was like floating on a sea of sensations. The orgasm just kept pounding, washing over her in wave after wave. His moves were slower, as if he wanted to prolong her delight.

By the time he gave over to his own body's demands, Genna had lost count of her orgasms. It wasn't until he slid out and moved away, then lay back down to pull her tight into his arms, that the sexual aftershocks started to abate.

Well. Nothing like incredible sex to clarify a few things.

Not that Genna had had incredible sex before tonight.

Mediocre, okay. Decent sex, yes. But tonight, Brody had shown her the difference between a nice orgasm and a mind-blowing, ongoing, multiclimaxing meltdown.

Her fingers tangled in the soft hair of his chest, she snuggled in closer and sighed. His scent wrapped around her as tightly as his arms, keeping her close, making her feel special.

Tonight had shown her what great sex was, yes. But it'd also made her realize that she'd been fooling herself that this thing she had for Brody was just a fun, easy thing to enjoy while he was home. Something she'd be able to look back on with a smile as a fond memory.

It'd been one thing to nurture a decade-old schoolgirl crush. To see him as a hero on a white horse who'd some-day ride in to sweep her into his arms. As someone who'd magically transform her life from blah to amazing with just a kiss.

That'd been a little silly, a lot sentimental.

So she had plenty of experience with what a crush felt like.

But now?

She'd had incredible sex, yes.

But she'd seen the real Brody. The man beneath the hero. The one who had fought hard to overcome an ugly beginning. Who had a sense of honor, of loyalty that was beyond her understanding of the words. A man who had made himself a real hero in the truest meaning of the word, but didn't see himself that way.

A man who could withstand all manner of pain, except the pain of feeling like he'd failed.

Finally, she felt as if she knew the real Brody.

And she was sure, absolutely and without any doubt, that she was 100 percent, head over heels in love with him.

And that—unlike the crush—was going to end up breaking her heart.

Genna snuggled in closer, trying to get as close to him as she could. As sexually fueled exhaustion pulled her down, her last thought was that whatever heartache she experienced, Brody was worth it.

11

WHO KNEW THAT a steady diet of cookies and mind-blowing sex could change a girl's life?

Three days of lovemaking, of sharing secrets and cuddling up with Brody, and she was a new woman.

A sexy, powerful, confident woman who could turn her big, bad SEAL into a panting puddle of lust with just the brush of her lips. Depending on where she brushed her lips, of course.

A strong woman who could handle anything. Including gossip, teasing and no shortage of envious looks from the women around town when they saw her with Brody.

A confident woman who knew what she wanted. Who was getting all kinds of brave and making the changes she'd dreamed of for years.

"You're sure of this?" Mayor Tucker asked, gesturing with the resignation letter in his hand. Standing in front of her table—her position didn't merit an actual desk—Genna followed his glance and took a deep breath.

But there were no nerves to chase away.

She felt incredible.

"I am. I've enjoyed working here and I'm grateful for the contacts I've made." Especially as they'd be such a big help to her starting her own business. "But I think it's time to move on."

"I'll wish you all the best in your new venture, then. As someone who's enjoyed your baking over the years, I have no doubt you'll be successful." Refolding the letter into a tidy rectangle, Tucker gave her a considering look. Then, using the same direct diplomacy that'd gotten him elected twice, he asked, "Have you thought through all of the ramifications of leaving, though? While I wish you the best and am sure most people will as well, some might be a bit concerned."

Genna's stomach clenched as the image of her father's furious face flashed through her imagination. Concern? Talk about an understatement. When her parents found out, they were going to have their own version of an all-out kicking and screaming tantrum.

She wasn't looking forward to it.

But neither was she going to let that kind of thing run her life. Not anymore.

"I know I'll have a few issues to overcome, but I'm sure I can handle them," she said, pretty much lying since she wasn't sure at all. But she wanted to be. And that was good enough for now. Especially since her father wasn't due back for another couple of days. Plenty of time to shore up her nerve and strengthen her spine.

Looking as though he wanted to say more, Tucker sighed, then nodded. Then, with a grimace, he offered, "If you need anything, just let me know. Business advice, a recommendation, a mediator."

Genna laughed.

"I'm glad you understand," she said, truly grateful that he was making it so easy. Then again, maybe he was looking forward to having her—and her interfering father—out of his office.

"You've been great. Even though this position wasn't

my idea, you've been a wonderful asset to the city. It'll be hard to replace you."

"Thank you." Genna hesitated, then figuring she had nothing to lose, she asked, "Can I ask a favor in return? I'll need permits and licenses."

"You want me to waive them?" Tucker asked, a small frown creasing his brow.

"Oh, no. I'll get them all like I'm supposed to. Just, well, can you make sure they don't get blocked?" She didn't need to add who the potential blocker would be. They both knew as soon as word of this got back to her father, he was going to make things ugly. She might need Tucker's mediation skills after all.

"I'll take care of it," the mayor assured her, patting her shoulder as he passed by. Then he stopped and turned with a frown. "One thing before you pack your bags. We need to finalize the arrangements for the hero appreciation day. Did you have any luck convincing our erstwhile military man to participate?"

Pleased that the event for Brody would be her last job here in the mayor's office, Genna pulled a folder from the stack in her tote.

"I've organized all of the vender donations, as well as coordinated with the high school band and the ladies' groups," she said, handing it to him. "As soon as we finalize the date I'll contact the sheriff's office to arrange to close off the pertinent streets. Custodial is already giving an extra polish to the town hall so it'll be ready for the luncheon."

Tucker gave an impressed nod.

"And you've got Lane on board with it?"

"Well, not exactly on board." Genna bit her lip. "But I think I can convince him."

As soon as she got the nerve to ask him again.

She was sure he'd say yes. Okay, almost sure. Sort of.

Maybe it'd help if she asked while they were naked.

He seemed to be willing to do anything she wanted then.

Tucker didn't look very assured. Given that he didn't know Genna's secret weapon, she couldn't blame him.

"I'll get a commitment," she promised.

"By tomorrow," the mayor prodded. "The press needs lead time to build some buzz. We want to be above the fold and it's going to be hard to top his being decorated by the president. See if he can get a few other SEALs to attend. That'd make great press."

Genna kept her smile in place while the mayor continued his excited recital of plans on his way to his office. At his door, he gave her a finger wag. "Tomorrow. Get it done."

She waited for his door to close before dropping her head into her hands.

Convince Brody to play hero. Do it by tomorrow. Build buzz and drag in a few extra SEALs for a more colorful photo op.

Easy peasy.

Genna's head snapped up when the front door ricocheted off the wall.

Her father strode in, looking as though he wanted to shoot somebody.

Guess he was back in town. And he was clearly up to speed on the gossip about his daughter's love life. She wondered how long it'd take before the hospital called.

"Hi, Dad," she greeted him, getting to her feet. No point letting him look down on her any further than she had to.

He barely glanced her way.

"Tucker in?"

"He is." Genna was tempted to let it go at that. He could have his powwow with the mayor, she could sneak out and start her new life. But that was the weenie way. So she cleared her throat and said in a rush, "But I need to speak to you before you go in."

"What's up?" The sheriff gave her a questioning look. "Tucker giving you a rough time? Working you too hard? Want me to talk to him?"

He'd do it, too. Go in there and tell the mayor of Bedford to quit picking on his little girl, the mayor's paid employee. Genna had always thought it kind of sweet, knowing she'd always be looked out for. But now it was stifling, like the very thought was choking all the air out of her life.

"Tucker's fine. But it is about my job," she said.

Then she ran out of words.

She wanted to ease into it. Make sure he understood how important this was to her. How excited she was about opening a bakery, that it was her dream job. If she could get that across first, then he'd take the news about her job much better.

A half smile on his face, her father arched one brow.

"Yeah? What about your job?"

"Um, I just quit." Well, Genna wrinkled her nose. That was eloquent. Any chance he'd clued in to how excited she was by her shaking tone?

"You what?" Looking as if he was going to burst a vein, he didn't wait for her to repeat the obvious. Instead he stabbed one finger toward the mayor's door. "Then get in there and ask for it back."

"I don't want it back," she said quickly, pushing the words through her nerves, knowing she had to take a stand or give up her dream altogether. "I quit because I'm going to bake full time."

Her father sighed. He took off his Sheriff ball cap, ran one hand through his still-thick hair as if trying to comb away a headache, and tugged the cap back on.

"Genna, we've discussed this." His tone shifted from angry to reasonable. So reasonable that Genna was almost nodding before he'd said another word. "You'd be dealing with complete strangers day in and day out. You'd have no stable income, no insurance, no sick pay. You simply don't have the experience or the knowledge to run your own business."

And he had no respect for her, Genna wanted to yell. But that'd get her nowhere.

"This isn't some impulsive craze," she defended instead. "I have a BA in business, and this is exactly what I studied for and it's time to make it happen. I'm calling it Sugar and Spice. I've made arrangements with the café and three of the restaurants in town to carry my desserts. Even Mr. Jenson is going to sell my cookies from the pharmacy. I've got orders already, enough to carry me through the first month, possibly three. Then I can look at getting a storefront."

A cute one over on Beeker, maybe. Right between the dress shop and the library. It'd get great foot traffic, plus there was a good-size parking lot across the street.

Summer, she promised herself. She'd be decorating her own shop by summer.

"When did you do all of this?" her father asked slowly, his fingers tapping on his belt as he frowned at her. "I've only been gone five days."

A girl could get a lot done in five days when she was motivated. And Genna was. She wanted this job. And more, she wanted to prove to Brody that she could make things happen. That she wasn't a wimpy little daddy's girl who couldn't stand on her own two feet.

"It's something I've been dreaming about for a long time. I've been making notes, sketching out ideas, for years. Once I decided it was time, it was pretty easy to do," she said, reaching into her tote for the expandable file folder filled with ideas, plans and orders that she'd shared earlier with the mayor.

She bit her lip, excited to see how impressed her dad would be with her work.

Before she could show him, though, he was shaking his head and giving her that cop look of his. The one that made a person want to confess to crimes they'd only thought of just to get him to look away.

"Have you been seeing Brody Lane?"

Genna pressed her lips together. Seeing, doing. Neither was something she wanted to discuss with her father. Especially given the way he felt about Brody.

She tried to settle the nerves gnawing their way through her stomach. She'd known word would get out. If Macy hadn't told—and surprisingly, she hadn't—someone else would have since she and Brody had been out in a lot more public places the last week or so.

"This has something to do with that troublemaker," her father accused, reading her face much too well. His wasn't tough to decipher either. Fury came across loud and clear.

"No. Starting a career is my decision, something I came to all on my own. It has nothing to do with Brody," Genna said quickly, her fingers knotted together to keep her hands from shaking. Well, it did. But not how her father meant. "This is my dream. It's something I've wanted for years."

"And you just happened to decide it was time to make it happen this week? When I was out of town?"

That had definitely made it a lot easier.

But Genna shook her head. "I had a house filled with baked goods to find homes for. The more people I shared with, the more people talked about how they'd buy from me, the more I couldn't see any reason to wait."

"I can think of plenty of reasons. You go talk to Tucker and get your job back. Then we'll sit down and go over this reasonably. You, your mother and me. If it's the best thing for you to do, we'll support you."

No, they wouldn't. They'd do exactly what they'd done

every other time she'd gone to them to share her plans. They'd talk her out of it. Or they'd guilt her out of it. One or the other.

"No," she said quietly. She untwined her hands, flexing her fingers once to shake off a little tension, then took a deep breath. "I've already made my decision."

"This is that damned Lane's fault," her father growled. "He's trouble. The only reason he didn't end up in jail is because the military had him locked down and under control."

"If he was as bad as you seem to think, he wouldn't have made it in the military as long as he did. Nor would he be a part of the elite Special Forces, or a decorated SEAL," she pointed out, trying to sound reasonable. She didn't want to come across as a defensive lover. That wasn't going to score points with her father.

"He's just as bad as your brother was. It's his fault Joe went the direction he did. That he found so much trouble and couldn't climb out."

Genna had to look away to clear the tears from her eyes. Not over her brother's path of self-destruction. He'd made that choice and she'd cried plenty about it over the years. But that her father was so blind to his part in Joe's choices. That he would blame someone else, someone who'd never been as bad as Joe, who'd been gone for the worst of Joe's hell-bent-to-worthless years.

"Brody isn't Joe. He never was." She didn't need to say that Joe had been raised with every privilege, often more than he'd appreciated. While Brody had been raised with nothing. No fancy toys or fast cars, no designer clothes or cool trips. Not even three healthy meals a day or a safe home. Or love. "And neither was I. But you punished me for Joe's actions. The worse he became, the less freedom I had."

Maybe because Joe blithely ignored every punishment

their parents set. Whereas Brody had taken her father's punishment and used it to build a life to be proud of. And that, she figured, said it all.

"I'm seeing Brody Lane. And I'll keep seeing him as long as I choose to," she told him quietly. Her nerves wound so tight, she felt like her hair was going to fly off. Her stomach churned, sick with nausea. But she kept her chin high and her eyes steady. "You can't run him off this time. You can't put me on restriction and take away my privileges."

"You'd be surprised at what I can and can't do." Looking every inch the cop he was, her father seemed to tower over her. Like a threat. Or a jail sentence.

Like a light flashing in the dead of night, the truth washed over her. All of a sudden, her head started spinning. She had to stop and breathe through the dizziness.

"That's what you've been doing all along, isn't it? You didn't like my choices, so you and Mother systematically took them away from me. You, with your rules and guidance. All along, you've kept me on restriction."

"You're being melodramatic."

"Am I? First it was college. Then you used your influence around town to make sure I stayed between those narrow lines you drew. I lived where you wanted, worked where you chose."

Sure, she'd realized her dad was a pain in the butt when it came to being overprotective. But until now, she'd refused to admit how bad he was. How much he'd restricted her every single freaking choice.

And the ones he'd somehow lost control of? Her mother swooped in to play the health card for the win.

How many people saw what she'd been so reluctant to face? Brody did. All his comments, his questions suddenly came into brilliant focus. He'd seen it. Her friends had commented from time to time. Even Macy, although her comments usually supported Genna's parents.

Brody had accused her of using him to rebel. She hadn't lied when she'd denied it, because she hadn't been brave enough to take that kind of risk.

But he was right. She had used him. The truth was, she'd used him to find herself again. It was only through Brody that she'd been able to reconnect with her own wants, her own needs. With her own self.

That she'd had to was demoralizing.

"Everything we did was for your own good, Genna." Still using his father-knows-best tone, her dad stepped forward as if to take her hands.

Genna stepped back.

His scowl made her want to add a few extra steps to her retreat.

"You can't run my life, Dad. Not anymore."

"I can, and will, do whatever I think is best for my family," her father shot back.

"You're so busy forcing your family to follow your rules, to fit your preconceived ideas, that you're destroying it." Genna swallowed hard to get past the tears clogging her throat. Her dad might be bossy and overprotective, but he was still her dad. She hated hurting him. But she couldn't—wouldn't—let him continue to run her life. "If you can't accept my choices, then maybe it's better if you just stayed away."

Her eyes blurred, she hurried past him and out the door before he could respond.

BRODY STEPPED INTO the room that'd once fit him like a second skin. This bunk, a cot in a tent, a rack on a ship. It didn't matter. They'd been home. Barracks were all the same. Coronado, Little Creek, Pearl Harbor or Afghanistan. He'd fit. He'd belonged.

Now?

He looked around the bland room, his gaze avoiding the bunk next to his. Carter's bunk.

Now he wasn't sure.

"Dude, you're back?"

Brody turned in time to catch Masters's hand in a tight shake and gave a half shrug.

"Just finished physical therapy."

"Finished a session? Or finished completely?" Masters asked, his green eyes intense.

"Both."

"Yeah? You're cleared for duty?"

"Gotta see the doctor on Monday. But the physical therapist said I'm solid."

"Nice timing. We ship out in a month, start training next week."

A week. Brody was silent. Genna's face flashed through his mind. What would she say if she knew? After that first night, they'd never talked about his service. For the first time, he realized they'd both been avoiding it.

"So what's the deal?" Masters asked, reading the stress in Brody's tone. "You thinking about opting out?"

"I don't quit."

"No. But if you can't give it one hundred percent, you're not an asset."

A brutal statement by some standards. But not Masters's. And not Brody's. He knew it was the truth. Their commander ran the team with a strong hand, demanding the best from each man, pushing them all to their limits, then shoving them right past to find new limits. A SEAL carrying baggage was a detriment. To himself. To the mission. To the team.

"So what's the deal?" Masters asked, grabbing a wooden chair and spinning it around before straddling it. He waited until Brody had done the same, then he picked up the deck of cards on the table between them and started shuffling. "You've been cleared of PTSD, right? You say you didn't B.S. your way through testing. So it's gotta be something else."

Brody debated while Masters dealt.

He wasn't a sharesies kind of guy. He didn't believe confession was good for the soul. And whatever nasty crap he had in the closets of his mind was just fine hiding out there. He'd lived through plenty of ugly in his life and ignored it all just fine.

So why was this different?

He lifted his cards, tossed one down.

"You ever question your ability to do your job?" he asked quietly, taking the new card Masters flipped across the table.

His buddy stared at his hand for a couple heartbeats. Brody knew he was thinking. The guy didn't say boo without considering all the ramifications. Finally, Masters looked up and gave a jerk of his shoulder.

"No. That's probably not what you want to hear, but it's the truth. We're the best. We do what nobody else can do. And we're damned good at doing it."

Brody nodded. He used to believe that, too.

"You questioning the job you did?" Masters asked, his words quiet as he rearranged his cards.

"I failed." There. He'd said it. Some people might think confessing their deepest shame was cathartic. Brody had news for them. It sucked. His gut ached and his head throbbed as he heard his own words.

He'd left Bedford a loser with little or no prospects. Ten years later, he was back and not much had changed. He still had the hots for the town princess. She was sneaking around seeing him on the sly. And his prospects? Pretty freaking lousy.

He met his friend's eyes with a shake of his head.

"My failure cost us a brother."

Masters pursed his lips, that computer brain probably replaying the mission statement and everyone's assignment, the operation itself, and the postmission assessment.

Then he shook his head.

"You saved a little girl. A kid who wasn't supposed to be in that compound. Despite spotty intelligence, you listened to her old man, went back in and found her, and hauled her out with a bullet in your thigh just before the place exploded all to hell. That's your job. You did it. What's the problem?"

"I wasn't the last man out."

Masters's face stiffened for a second, his jaw tight. He gave a short nod.

"Carter went down. It happens, man. We all know that going in."

"He took a chunk of concrete to the back. He went down fast, but he was alive. I should have grabbed him then," Brody said, staring at the cards in his hand but not seeing them. Instead, images flashed of that mission. Of his friend's face, fire flaring all around them, the air filled with concrete as sharp as shrapnel.

"You had an injured kid in your arms and a damaged leg. You were ordered to get her out."

"I almost went back. I could have carried them both. She was hardly more than a handful. But she was terrified. Started screaming and crying when I turned back. I figured I'd drop her at the helo, go back and get Carter."

"That's SOP."

"The building blew before I could get back."

"It blew before any of us could get back." Masters's words were toneless, easy. But Brody heard the pain in them. Knew the guy was struggling with his own demons. They'd all had a job to do, had all been focused on getting it done. But they should have gotten Carter out.

"No man left behind." Brody's jaw clenched so tight he had to force the team slogan past gritted teeth. "I failed."

"If you'd gone back, you and the kid would have gone down, too. You got out of there with five seconds to spare."

"I should have grabbed him."

"Did you show the president the big fat *S* on your chest when he pinned you with that medal?" Masters asked, rolling his eyes and laying down a straight. "I thought your call sign was Bad Ass. Not Superman."

Despite the misery curled in his gut, Brody smirked.

"Talk it out, hit the gym, visit the range," Masters suggested, folding his arms over the back of the chair and meeting Brody's gaze. "But get over it."

"You been reading psych books again?"

Masters didn't smile. Instead, he slid his cards together, tapped them on the table a couple of times, then met Brody's eyes. His own gaze was steady, rock-solid.

"I'm damned choosy about who I serve with. About who I trust to cover my back. I'd serve with you without question," the guy said, his words too matter-of-fact to be taken as sappy or sentimental. "I have complete confidence, not only in your ability to do your job. But in the simple fact that if I go down, you'll do everything in your power to get me out. I can't offer up a higher trust than that."

They were SEALs. Bred for action. Words were rarely necessary, and other than to geeks like Masters who obsessed with books the way some guys drooled over porn, they didn't mean much.

But hearing his teammate's trust, knowing the guy wouldn't hesitate to take the field with him again, it went a long way to bridging that gaping hole inside Brody. The one he could no longer ignore.

"Thanks." Taking a deep breath, Brody faced the decision that'd been lurking for the last two months, waiting for him to man up. "But until I know it, too, I'm no good to the team."

Brody laid down his cards, stood and clapped his buddy on the shoulder, and strode out of the room.

Just before he hit the door, he heard Masters mutter, "Son of a bitch. Royal flush? Does he ever lose?"

12

So this was what life was like without daily PT, constant training and an ongoing need to challenge himself to push the limits. No missions, no range practice, no combat.

It was sort of mellow.

Settled on Genna's couch with her curled up at his feet working on her latest brainstorm, Brody watched familiar scenes flash on the television.

Mellow was an odd speed for him. He wasn't sure how he felt about it yet.

For ten years, he'd been going at full tilt.

The nineteen years before that had been spent on edge. Always ready to fight, always ready to run.

The last few months felt like turmoil.

But maybe, this week, he'd found peace. Or at least now that he'd pretty much decided his future, he wasn't battling his own brain. That was close enough to peace, wasn't it?

The irritating nag of a million doubts ran through his mind, mocking him. Okay, so he wasn't at peace. So what. It wasn't as if he'd ever been before.

He was happy, though.

His gaze shifted from the bomb-ravaged scene on the TV to the woman sitting at his feet.

Genna's hair gleamed like black silk in the lamplight. He could only see her profile, but had to smile at the way her lips were moving as she made silent comments about whatever she was writing. Her enthusiasm, her whole-hearted excitement over her new business, was pretty awesome. She didn't let the obstacles, the issues with her family or the various questions he'd heard tossed her way slow her down. This was her dream and by damn, she was going to make it happen.

She was his dream, he realized.

Not just the hot sweaty kind. Although she'd ratcheted those up a few notches over the last couple of weeks. He'd never been a man who shied away from great sex, but clearly he'd been clueless to just what great was.

But Genna was more.

Sweet and fun, she believed in him. She gave him a feeling of contentment, of happiness, he'd never had. Never even knew existed.

As if clueing in that he was thinking about her, she flashed him a smile.

"Mr. Jenson said you and he had a fun chat today," she said, looking up from where she was cozied between his thighs in front of the coffee table. She had a slew of papers spread over the surface, notes and sketches, at least three calendars and God knew what else. But it seemed to be making her happy. And that's what he wanted. Her, happy.

"I stopped in the pharmacy to pick up my gramma's prescription and he wanted to talk. I guess there aren't too many people to share his Korean War stories with."

"Well, there is the VFW and the American Legion. But everyone there has heard his stories. You're fresh blood. And you've got rock star status, being a SEAL and all," she teased.

Brody hoped she'd take his grimace as a smile.

Rock star.

Right.

That'd change in a heartbeat once word got out that he was leaving the navy. He'd be back to being a loser and deadbeat in everyone's eyes. Except Genna's. Which was all that he was going to let matter. He'd rather see the relief in her gaze than the worry he figured would be there if she had to see him leaving on mission after mission.

"How are the business plans shaping up?" he asked, wanting to change the subject.

"I'd thought it'd take a lot longer for word to get out that I'd started Sugar and Spice. I mean, I know this is mostly curiosity and test orders. It'll level out in a month or so. I just hope it doesn't level too much lower," she mused, looking at a list of potential restaurants that were interested in carrying her desserts. "Or that my father would intimidate people out of ordering from me so I'd have to climb back under his thumb. I'm setting up a website. You know, a lot of bakers are having big success with next-day orders. And that way, even if my dad scares away locals, I'm still in good shape."

Good plan. Then, his brows furrowed, he hit the pause button to freeze Jeremy Renner on the screen.

Would her old man really go that far?

"Have you talked to him at all?"

"My dad? Not since I told him I'd quit my job." Genna shrugged. "But I have heard from the mayor four times this week."

"He wants you to come back to work for him?"

"More like he wants me to talk you into changing your mind about being the guest of honor for his Honoring Our Heroes event," she said, making it sound like a joke.

Brody's jaw clenched and something ugly churned in his gut. Not happening.

But he'd already told her that a dozen times, so he didn't bother repeating himself.

As if sensing his irritation, Genna shifted onto his lap. Liking how she fit there, he wrapped his arms around her waist, but his frown didn't budge.

"You going to be okay with this?"

"With what? Sitting on your lap? Or playing messenger for the mayor?" she asked with a teasing smile.

He didn't give a damn about the mayor.

"With the crap from your parents. I don't like you taking heat for seeing me."

Her sigh was a work of art, complete with a roll of those pretty blue eyes and a tap of her fingernails against his shoulder. Damn, she was cute.

"My father isn't punishing me for seeing you," she finally said. "I told you, I'm the one who told him to stay away unless he could accept my career decision. Not the other way around."

"Are you thinking he'll try scare tactics when the freeze-out doesn't work?"

"Maybe," she said with a shrug. "But I told you, I've already figured out how to counter it if he does. I bartered a cake with a gal who does web design for her son's graduation. She's already working on an online store for me."

"Look, I don't want you to worry about the money stuff or let it slow down your progress. I know you're set for the next few months, but if you run into trouble, let me know. I can help out." He might not have a clue what he was doing with his life, any idea of where he fit in the world now or even where he'd be sleeping in six months.

But if he could help Genna make her dream come true, he figured he was set.

HE WANTED TO HELP HER?

"You're serious?" she breathed.

It wasn't a proposal, or a big emotional declaration. To Genna, it was even more. It was a promise that he'd be around. That they had a future, whatever that might look like.

Her heart melted in her chest, warm, soft and gooey. Unable to resist, she wrapped her arms around his shoulders and hugged him tight.

Her smile was wide enough to split her face when she pulled away to brush a quick kiss over his lips. Then, happier than she could remember, she shook her head.

"No, but thank you."

"What? Why not?" Brody scowled.

"That is the sweetest offer and I appreciate it." Probably more than he wanted. But that was just one more reason she was madly in love with him. And yet another reason to be careful to protect herself. It was enough that her heart counted on him. She couldn't risk her business, too. "But you stepped in to save me once. I don't want that to be the basis for our relationship, you know?"

"I thought the basis for our relationship was sex," he teased.

"Exactly," she said with a relieved laugh. "Why mess with a good thing?"

He nodded, but the serious look didn't leave his eyes. "Fine. You go it alone. But if you run into trouble, let me help you. I've got plenty saved up. I can afford to buy my way into a lifetime supply of cookies to keep you from losing your dream."

Her eyes soft, she reached out to cup his cheek in one hand and kiss him again.

"You are so sweet," she said when she lifted her lips from his.

"The hell I am."

He looked so embarrassed, she decided to give him a break and change the subject.

"Did you want to see the site design?" Shuffling papers,

she grabbed the sketch pad. "Maybe tell me what you think of the colors and logo we're doing?"

"You're kidding, right?" Brody gave her a pained expression. "You want a taste tester, I'm your guy. But you start talking colors and decorations and crap, I'm outta here."

"I've been horrible, haven't I?" she said with a laugh, tossing the sketch pad aside. "Not only do I keep asking you all these questions you have no interest in answering, but I've had you try every recipe I've made in the last week."

"Well, you've kept me pretty well compensated," he mused, that sexy glint in his eyes making Genna shiver. She loved how he looked at her. As if she were the key to his every sexual fantasy.

"Would you like a little compensation right now?" she asked in a teasing tone, shifting so she was straddling his body, her hands anchored on the couch behind his head.

"Sounds good," he murmured against her throat. His kisses sent shivers through her, but it was the hot rod pressing against his zipper that had her all kinds of excited.

"What'd you have in mind?" she said, sliding against his erection in a slow, undulating move that was making it hard to breathe.

"A cookie."

What? Genna pulled back to look at him. His smile was as huge as the hard length pressing against her aching core. Laughing, she leaned in to kiss him, reveling in the taste and texture of his mouth before shifting back just a little.

"You can have a cookie afterward," she promised.

Before she could get started, though, his cell phone rang. As much for the fun of wiggling in his lap as to be helpful, she reached around to grab it off the side table.

"I've already had my way with you once today," she

said, placing a teasing kiss on his chin. "Go ahead and take your call. I'll compensate you afterward."

"No."

Brody stared at the readout. The phone went silent, then black before he blinked, then tossed it onto the coffee table. It bounced twice before skidding into the popcorn bowl. Genna tensed, looking at the phone, then back at Brody's face. He didn't appear angry. Just distant.

"Is everything okay?" she asked quietly. She didn't want to pry. But she couldn't ignore how upset he seemed.

"Fine." He blinked, and it was as if she'd imagined the closed look on his face. In its place now was a cheerfully charming smile.

She frowned.

Brody didn't do cheerful.

Something was definitely wrong.

"That was Blake," he said, giving a first name to the "Lt. Landon" she'd seen on the screen. "He's got some irritating mother-hen tendencies."

"So he's calling to check on you?"

"Probably." Brody shrugged. "I don't feel like talking, though."

Shock. Brody Lane didn't want to talk?

Genna knew she should ignore her nagging sense of worry. But since she doubted his teammate was calling to discuss feelings, relationships or their rocky past, she couldn't. Not when he looked so unhappy. But whatever was bothering him, she knew he wouldn't share.

So maybe she should ask about what was bothering her. Nervous, but knowing she'd never get a better opportunity, she swallowed hard and forced herself to say, "So… You'll be going back soon."

He grunted. She took it as a yes.

"I know you don't get to say where you'll live or how long you're in any one place." And it wasn't as if she was asking to follow him around. Although she would if he asked. "Do you think, maybe once in a while between missions. If, you know, you're stationed at Coronado. If, maybe, you'd come back and visit?"

Genna mentally cringed. The only way she could sound more hesitant and unsure was if she'd thrown in a whining tone with all those maybes.

Brody didn't cringe, though. Nor did he get that distant look that told her she'd stepped into classified territory. Instead, he gave her a long stare, then smiled.

She wasn't sure why the smile made her want to cry.

"I've got some career options ahead. I've decided not to re-up in May. I'd be leaving the navy. So maybe instead of visiting, we can just see each other all the time."

Genna stared, her mind spinning.

She'd hoped, in that way-back secret corner of her mind, that the option of an online business would make it easier for her to keep her dream if she just so happened to be following Brody from base to base.

But now Brody was leaving the navy? He was moving back. And he wanted a relationship with her. Not just a "distance, naughty letters, and the occasional phone call or conjugal visit" kind of a relationship. But a day-in-and-day-out one.

She wasn't sure if she should giggle, jump up and down with happiness, or freak out.

"You cool with this?" he said after a solid minute of her mindless staring.

Genna yanked herself out of the reverie, starting to smile. Like a blooming flower, joy spread through her bright and shiny. The smile turned to a grin, then into a giggle.

For the second time that evening she threw her arms around his neck, hugging him close while the giddy laughter poured through her.

"Cool with it?" she asked, so excited she'd have bounced in his lap if she wasn't worried about damaging anything she was going to want to celebrate with soon. "I'm so happy and so excited. I love you so much."

She froze.

Her smile disappeared and the giggles fled.

No. She wanted to grab those words back. Her mind raced, trying to think of some way to play them off, or something to say that'd be shocking enough to make him forget she'd said that. But she couldn't come up with anything more outrageous than blurting out her love.

Cringing, she watched Brody's face.

Instead of looking distant, though, his eyes softened.

He ran one hand through her hair, his fingers tangling in the strands by her ear as he pulled her mouth to his. The kiss was so soft, so sweet, Genna swore they were floating on a cloud. Fear fled, worry faded. All that was left was the most intense sense of happiness.

Brody shifted, so she was on her back on the couch and he was poised over her. Their clothes disappeared between kisses, their breath mingled, quickening as their hands slid over each other. Except for the time it took to slip on a condom, Brody's mouth never left hers.

Fully embedded, he slowly pulled away to meet her gaze, his expression filled with the same emotions she felt churning through her.

Then he started moving. Slow and sweet.

And whispered, "I love you, too."

So this was what it felt like to have your dreams come true. Brody loved her. And he was happy that she loved him. Even in her favorite fantasies over the years, she'd always figured that if she ever accidentally let that slip, he'd run faster than a bullet left a gun.

But he hadn't. He'd smiled. He'd said he loved her back.

And then he'd made the sweetest love to her as if in testament to their words. It was the most amazing feeling. As if someone had reached inside her heart and lit the happiness light as bright as it could be.

She looked at the pages spread over the table, the tidy list of orders color-coded by type and arranged by date. She'd spent the morning on the phone with wholesale suppliers, thrilled to be able to rattle off her business information and place orders.

She should be ecstatic.

Sure, her father wasn't talking to her. They'd actually passed on the street the day before and he'd pointedly looked the other way. It was almost funny. In a *holy crap, are you kidding with the immaturity* kind of way.

And yes, her mother was calling daily to keep Genna in the health-crisis loop. The hospital trips, a migraine and a cold in the last week. Her last message had included a warning that if Genna didn't do something about her stress-inducing behavior, she'd be forced to take drastic measures. Since she hadn't included details on what those measures might include, Genna had ignored it.

Because her business rocked and her love life was a dream come true.

Well, to be precise, her business had the potential to rock, if it didn't fall apart. And while her sex life was amazing and her heart was happy, there was something nagging in the back of her head.

Brody was leaving the navy?

Why?

She'd asked, but all he'd say was that it was time.

That was good, right?

It'd be so much easier to have a relationship with someone who was actually around, instead of off fighting secret missions most of the time. He'd be safer here. Nobody would try to blow him up or shoot his leg full of holes. The only secrets he'd have to protect were her recipes.

That was good.

Wasn't it?

The doorbell chimed, loud and distracting.

Grateful for the interruption, Genna almost ran for the door, her stockinged feet sliding on the hardwood. Please, let it be someone with an elaborate baking order that would require a lot of focus and attention. Or anyone she wasn't related to who didn't want to talk about her family issues.

She pulled the door open to a blast of cold air and a total stranger. Frowning, she shifted her grip on the door so it'd be easy to slam if necessary.

The guy looked as if he could be plenty dangerous, but he didn't appear to be a threat. Supershort brown hair, blue eyes and a friendly smile, she mentally cataloged as her father'd taught her. About six foot wearing jeans, a black turtleneck and a leather bomber jacket.

Nope, he didn't look like a threat. But he didn't look like he was there to order a cake, either.

"Hi?"

"Hi." His gaze was laser sharp, the inspection quick and impersonal. Still, it left Genna feeling as if he'd just accessed all her secrets, her entire history and her driving record. "I'm Blake Landon. I'm looking for Brody. His grandmother said I might find him here."

Ahh. Genna's frown shifted to a smile. The SEAL friend who kept calling Brody.

"He's not here right now. But I expect him soon. Did you want to leave a message?" She relaxed her grip, letting the door swing open a little more.

Dark brows creased, the guy gave a quick glance over his shoulder at the BMW parked in front of Genna's house. She followed his gaze to see a woman in the passenger seat. Seeing their attention, the redhead gave a friendly wave.

"My wife and I were hoping to see him. Can you suggest a restaurant or bar in the area? We'll grab a bite to eat and come back in an hour or so."

It was three in the afternoon on a Thursday. Too late for lunch, too early for dinner at any place worth recommending. Genna debated for all of two seconds before waving back, then gesturing to her entryway.

"I'm really not sure how long Brody will be, and all I have to serve are desserts. But if you'd like, you're both welcome to wait here."

He gave her another one of those laser looks, this one a little more personal with a hint of curiosity. Then he nodded and turned, gesturing for his wife to join them.

"Alexia would like that. She's a fan of all things dessert. And of Brody's. So be warned, she's going to ask a million nosy questions."

A million?

Before Genna could reconsider, the redhead joined them. Gorgeous and leggy, she wore stunning knee-high black leather boots, jeans and a white wool coat.

"Hi. I'm Alexia. And you must be Genna." The woman's friendly smile negated all of Genna's worries. "I'm so happy to meet you. Brody is one of my favorite people, so I know you will be, too."

Suddenly at ease, Genna smiled at the friendly enthusiasm and invited them both inside. Within minutes, they were seated around the table. The coffee on, Genna brought plates and a tray of cookies and tarts over.

"Oh, these look wonderful." Humming a little, Alexia considered her choices. Then, her plate gratifyingly full, she gave Genna a brilliant smile.

"So, let's chat. You can tell us all the great backstory on Bad Ass, and we'll bring you up to speed on the last few years."

"Did you just call Brody a badass?" Genna asked, not sure if she should laugh or be horrified.

"It's his call sign," Blake told her quietly, getting up and helping himself to coffee. "It seemed to fit."

Didn't it just.

"What's yours?" she asked.

Pausing in the act of pouring for all three of them, Blake looked her way and grinned. "Boy Scout."

Genna looked at Alexia, who rolled her eyes again and gave a little shake of her head. So Blake might always be prepared, but if his wife was to be believed, he was anything but a goody-goody.

"You want to know what Brody was like growing up?" Genna asked, trying not to imagine just how ungoody-goody Alexia could coax Blake to be.

"No secrets," Blake insisted. "Don't invade Brody's privacy."

Alexia rolled her eyes, her mouth too full to talk. Blake looked uncomfortable, as if dishing dirt on his teammate and friend was something he'd only tolerate because he adored his wife.

Genna liked him all the more for that.

"Well…" she said, drawing out the word to its fullest impact while she chose a pecan tart with caramel swirls. Inspecting the golden-brown perfection of it for a second, she raised her eyes and gave Alexia her best gossip face.

"Growing up, everyone in town called Brody a badass."

Alexia looked blank for one second, then she burst into laughter. Blake, on the other hand, just looked satisfied as he finally took a cookie. As if Genna had passed some secret test.

"Fair enough," Alexia said, exchanging glances with her husband. Genna envied how they seemed to have an entire conversation between blinks. "So maybe we'll chat about the SEALs instead. Do you have any family in the military?"

Genna set her half-eaten tart back on her plate and shook her head. "No. My father's in law enforcement, though. I know it's not the same, but there is a similar sense of service and focus, I think."

"There is," Alexia agreed. "It's not just a job, it's who they are. Their identity, their purpose. In a way, it's their life."

Genna frowned at the ease of the other woman's words.

"Doesn't that bother you just a little? I mean, not that I don't appreciate what you do," she told Blake, who didn't seem at all offended. Then she looked back at Alexia. "But if your husband's entire world is the military, where do you fit in?"

Alexia's eyes sparkled as if Genna had just asked the perfect question. If she'd been a teacher, she'd have pulled out a gold star.

"No, no. I said the military was his purpose. I'm his world," she said with absolute confidence. "But I'm not his priority. Not while he's on duty, at least."

The smile the couple shared told Genna that Alexia had no problem demanding all of Blake's attention when he wasn't on duty, though.

"And you're okay with that?" Genna asked, wondering if she could be.

"I wasn't at first," Alexia said quietly, her fingers curling over her husband's. "I grew up a military brat and was carrying a lot of baggage about it. But even without that, it takes a special woman to be able to handle the secrets, the risks and the long separations. To be able to build a life that fulfills her, but is still dedicated to a long-distance marriage. Military men are strong, but their women are stronger."

"Really?" Genna's laugh was a little skeptical, but she couldn't help it.

"Really," Blake said, answering for his wife.

She glanced back and forth between the couple, realizing that there was more than one kind of strength. And wondering if she had the kind it took to wait for her man, knowing he was in danger, knowing his duty came first.

"And it's just that easy?" she wondered.

"Hell, no."

"Of course not," Alexia said at the same time. She and Blake exchanged smiles. "But no marriage is easy. Nothing worthwhile in life is, really. But it's special enough, and we're strong enough, to make it work."

Genna tried to absorb that. She and Brody weren't even close to talking marriage. And he was leaving the navy, so it didn't matter if she wasn't strong enough to be a military wife or not. Did it? Or was that why he was leaving? Was it significant that he told her he loved her and that he was leaving the navy at the same time?

"You're wondering why I'm telling you this," Alexia guessed.

"Well, yeah." And when they were done, maybe they could tell her what to do, too. An ironic hope, since she'd spent years trying to get people to *stop* telling her what to do.

Alexia leaned forward, her face intent as she searched Genna's. Then, apparently liking whatever she found there, she said, "We want you to help us figure out how to convince Brody not to quit the SEALs."

13

FUELED BY GUILT over talking about Brody behind his back, and a stomachache from too many tarts, Genna pulled into the dingy parking of Slims. She'd been searching for Brody for the last two hours, and while she couldn't imagine why he'd want to come here, it was the last place inside city limits she could think of to look.

Parking next to a patch of weeds as tall as the bumper of her car, she puffed out a breath. She hated going in there. Not just because it was three shades of sleazy with a whole lot of gross on the side. But because it seemed to be the epitome of Brody's late father. Ugly, mean and under many circumstances, plain dangerous.

But two o'clock on a Friday afternoon shouldn't be bad. She hoped.

Steeling herself, and making sure her Mace was in her pocket, she slid from the car and crossed the gravel lot. She was careful to avoid the multitude of oil leaks—apparently the clientele at Slims wasn't big on auto maintenance. Pushing the scarred wooden door open, she stopped short inside to let her eyes adjust to the dim light.

Chairs stacked on tables gave testament that someone had at least pretended to clean the floor. The neon signs behind the bar glowed blurrily through a sea of dust motes. Floodlights similar to those she had in her back garden were lit and aimed toward the stage, if that's what they called the three pallets pushed together in the corner in front of the mike.

But there weren't any bodies.

Genna considered, then bent low to squint under the tables.

Nope. No bodies.

Dammit. She bit her lip, not sure where to look next. His Harley was still at his gramma's. So he had to be in town somewhere. Didn't he? Maybe she should just go home and wait for him.

Except the conversation with Blake and Alexia kept playing through her head, urging her to find him as quickly as possible.

They thought Brody leaving the SEALs was a big mistake. That he was doing it for the wrong reasons, even though neither of them had been willing to tell her what they felt his reasons were.

She knew, though.

When he'd lost his friend on that last mission, he'd lost his faith in his ability to do the job he expected from himself.

What she didn't know was what to do about that. Trying to help him through the emotional issue was pointless. She knew from experience dealing with her father and brother over the years that since she wasn't a SEAL, wasn't military and wasn't a guy, she wasn't qualified to try to talk him out of whatever he was feeling.

Until her visitors today, she'd figured that all she could do was be here, support him and then when he was ready to finally talk, listen.

But now she knew she had to do more. She couldn't let

him walk away from something so important to him unless he was really sure.

Unless he had already thought it through and *was* sure.

And as much as she'd always dreamed of Brody being in her life, she didn't want it to be at the expense of his own dreams. But if it was something he wanted to do just because, well. that was different.

She shoved both hands through her hair and tried not to scream at the conflicting thoughts battling it out for top spot in her mind.

Then she heard a noise. Her heart skipped. The scraping sounded again off the room behind the bar. Balanced on the tips of her toes, she shifted to run out the door.

Then she heard voices.

Brody?

Panic fled, leaving a frown as she stepped cautiously toward the bar.

As if her movement triggered a signal, Brody and Leon, the bar owner, stepped out. Leon looked bored, as usual. Brody's face flashed with surprise, then something that seemed like irritation that went too fast for her to be sure before he gave her a questioning look.

"Genna? Why are you here?"

"I was looking for you," she said, figuring that should be obvious. Her boots sticking to the floor in places, more proof that the chairs on the tables were a fake-out, she made her way across the room.

With each step, tension drained away, both from discomfort of being alone in such a sleazy setting, and from her worry over where Brody had disappeared to. Leaving plenty of room to wonder about why he'd disappeared to here. She'd think it'd be the last place he'd want to see.

"I got stuff to run to the bank. You cover for me?" Leon

mumbled, tucking a grungy sack into the front of his pants, then buttoning his flannel over it.

At Brody's nod, the older man skirted the bar and left, not glancing once toward Genna.

Even though she was apparently invisible to him, she still waited until the door closed before reaching across the scarred bar to give Brody's hand a squeeze.

Before she could say anything, he asked again, "Why are you here?"

"I told you, I was looking for you."

"I've got a cell phone." His words were short, his expression stiff. "Just call. Don't come looking, especially at a place like this."

Since she didn't like seeing him in a place like this, she couldn't blame him for feeling the same. But still, why was he here? Given the history, that his father spent most of Brody's life here drinking himself to death, you'd think he'd want to stay clear of it, too. Her frown deepened and she glanced at the small room behind the bar, then at the hand-lettered bartender-wanted sign on the stool.

She'd turned her life upside down and quit her job. She'd faced off with her father and offered her mother a silver platter full of health woe excuses. Thanks to Brody, she'd found the nerve to finally move forward with her life.

Her stomach knotted and bile rose in her throat.

And what? Thanks to her, he'd moved back?

She gazed around the dingy bar, the sense of desolation and despair as real as the dust and dirt. Back to this?

She was pretty sure when Prince Charming had ridden in to save the princess, he hadn't give up the castle to end up in a hovel.

As much as she hated to mess with what had this morning been a pretty awesome outlook for her life, they had to talk. She had to know, for sure, that he was going to be happy with his decision.

Otherwise, she thought as her heart sank into the toes of her sticky-soled boots, there was no hope for them to be happy together.

"BRODY, SERIOUSLY. WHAT are you doing here?"

Brody scowled. How the hell had she found him? He suddenly felt dirty. As though every nasty memory he'd had of this place was crawling over him. He figured he'd better get used to it, though.

"Leon had been bugging me to stop by and clear out the old man's stuff."

Genna moved closer, standing on tiptoes and making a show of trying to see over the bar.

"His stuff is back there?"

"You heard Leon. He asked me to man the bar for a half hour."

Her face as distant as he'd ever seen it, Genna took a deep breath, crossed her arms over her chest and gave him a long look. He damn near shuffled his feet, her eyes were so intense. It was as if she was looking inside him. As if she was checking out all his secrets.

He hoped she had plenty of time. He had a helluva lot of them.

"I heard Leon was looking for a new bartender."

"So?"

"So. Did you take the job?"

Shit.

Brody had spent most of his life answering to nobody. The last ten years answering to the navy. He'd sorta thought this round he'd answer only to himself.

He'd sorta thought wrong. At least, he had if he wanted Genna in his life.

And he did.

More than anything, more than everything, he wanted Genna. Even if it meant trying to justify his decisions.

Even the ones he couldn't quite come to terms with himself.

"I've gotta work," he said, irritated that he sounded so defensive. "Look, this is a good thing."

Her mouth dropped open and she blinked a couple of times, then shook her head as if clearing a buzz from her ears.

"A good thing? You, quitting the navy. Giving up being a SEAL. To what? Tend bar in the same sleazy dive you grew up over? Why? You missed all the happy memories?"

Damn. She had a smart mouth on her when she wanted. And a wicked way of kicking her point home right where it'd hurt most.

"Well, there's not a whole lot of jobs in Bedford requiring a sniper." He shrugged. "I'm trained to fight. To perform covert operations and carry out military strategies. Believe it or not, those skills aren't big moneymakers in the civilian world."

"But they are skills you love. Skills you're proud of." She lifted both hands in a classic WTF gesture. "So why are you throwing them away to pour drinks for drunks?"

Brody ground his teeth together to keep the cusswords from spewing out. Yeah. She was aces when it came to the well-aimed shot. This one didn't hit his ego, though. It went straight for the gut.

What a deal. Giving up a life of excitement, adrenaline and power to schlep booze for drunks. Traveling the world to hole up in the town he'd spent most of his life trying to escape. But that was his problem. And he was willing to do it if it meant a life with Genna.

Why was *she* pushing this? Most women, outside the frog hogs as the guys called the SEAL groupies, wanted a guy who was around. Who was around for Friday night dates, holidays and more days in the month than he was gone.

Maybe she just didn't get it.

"Look, this is a good thing. You should be happy," he said, despite the fact that she appeared about as far from that as he'd ever seen her. "This means I'm sticking around. You get that, right? That I'm here, that we can be together. No deployment, no long missions, no part of my life locked up and labeled classified."

Her eyes softened and some of the tension left her posture. For a second, he thought he had her. But Brody knew better than to relax.

"I want to be with you," she said, her words soft and sweet to match her smile. She stepped forward, taking his hands in hers and lifting one to her cheek.

Brody wasn't a mushy kind of guy. But that move, it slayed him. Especially when she was looking up at him as though he was her whole world and she was ready to love every second of it.

Then, with a quick brush of her lips over his knuckles, she released him and shook her head.

"You can't do it, though. You can't quit being who you are. You won't be happy."

"I'd be with you. That'd make me happy." Happy enough, he promised himself. The two of them building on what they had. That'd be enough. He'd make it enough.

Her eyes so bright they lit up even the dim dust of the bar, Genna smiled. But there was a line between her brows that got deeper as her smile faded. Slowly, she shook her head.

"I want to be with you. So much. I love you," she finally said. Her words sent a thrill through Brody. Not because they were some he'd rarely heard in his life. But because they came from her. And they meant everything.

"But you can't put that on me. I can't be the reason you leave the military. I can't fill the hole it's going to leave in your life."

"I'm not leaving because of you."

"But you're not leaving because you want to."

Brody scrubbed his hands over his face. God, this was stupid. Why the hell was she arguing with him? For a brief second, he missed the navy so much it hurt. For no other reason than in the navy, when someone issued an order or made a decision, everyone shut the hell up and accepted it.

"Look, I've made up my mind. I'm through. I can't be a SEAL anymore. And if I can't be a SEAL, I won't serve." He gestured to the bar. "This is a job. It's honest work and will pay the bills until I figure out what I want to do."

Honest work to pay the bills. It took Brody a moment to figure out why the words tasted so bitter. Then he remembered his father yelling them at his mother. Every argument they had over his drinking, his living at the bar, had ended with that statement.

Apparently they sounded just as good to Genna as they did to him.

"So this is it?" The wave of her hand was more a slap at the bar than an encompassing gesture. "Your future? Tending bar, holing up in that dingy apartment filled with ugly memories and despair?"

"Leon already rented out the dingy apartment. I figured I'd live with you." Clearly not in a joking mood, she just hissed. So he shrugged and amended that to, "Or in the guesthouse behind my grandmother's."

Her glare was just as threatening as an AK-47, making it clear she wasn't interested in smart-ass responses.

Okay, fine. She wanted the truth, she could find a way to deal with it.

"My future was being a navy SEAL. I worked my ass off for that, Genna. I trained for it, I lived it, I breathed it. I was it. And now I'm not." Brody glared right back, hating that she was forcing him to say the words aloud. "So excuse me if I make the best of the lousy hand I've been dealt."

She gave him a long look, then slowly nodded.

The vicious knots of tension gripping Brody's gut eased a little. Good. Maybe now she'd let it go.

"You don't have to take this deal. You have plenty of other options, including returning to duty."

Why? He wanted to drop his head into his hands and give it a good shake. Why did he ever believe she'd take the easy path? The one that tidily avoided all that emotional crap.

"What in the hell do you know about it?"

"Blake and Alexia came to see me earlier," she said. "I know your friend said the surgeon cleared you to go back to the navy. That the decision to leave the SEALs was yours."

If she'd hauled an Uzi from under her skirt and shot him, he couldn't have been more stunned.

Blake and Alexia had been in Bedford? Specifically to visit Genna, obviously. What the hell? Since when was it the lieutenant's job to play retention officer? Why did he care? Didn't he realize the team was better off this way? That any team was better off with a solid group of dependable men?

Brody didn't let any of that show on his face, though.

Any sign of weakness, of surprise, and she'd never let it go.

"Landon was right. It's my decision. And I decided to stay here."

"So… What? You're just going to spend the rest of your life here at Slims, pouring drinks and hiding from life? You really are taking Brian's place, aren't you?"

Her implication was like a slap to the face. He wasn't his old man. He wasn't a bitter, angry asshole who loved his booze more than anything else in his life.

He was just a bitter, angry asshole.

"I don't drink." Brody almost rolled his eyes at that

stupid statement. He was really hitting the bottom of the barrel on pathetic now.

"No? Why not?"

"My body is a military machine. A tool for Uncle Sam. You don't take care of your tools, they don't do the job they're supposed to. Alcohol dulls the senses, it slows reaction times. I'm not messing up hours of intense training for a cheap buzz."

His words trailed off as he realized he was speaking in the present tense. But his body wasn't finely tuned anymore. And his mind was jacked-up trash.

That realization crashed down on him along with the full impact of how hard he'd worked, how long he'd striven to be the best, to finally be someone people admired. Gone.

All fucking gone.

Brody didn't even realize he'd grabbed the whiskey bottle until the scent of Jim Beam hit him.

His eyes cut to Genna's.

Instead of the appreciation and understanding he'd grown used to seeing in those warm blue depths, this time there was contempt.

His gaze cut away, focusing on the whiskey hitting a dingy glass.

"Well," she said quietly. "I guess you have made your decision. You're going to turn your back on a career you apparently loved. One you're so good at, the president of the United States acknowledged you. One you've made such a difference in, the mayor of Bedford is throwing an event in your honor."

Was she still harping on that? The entire team was up for the Silver Star, not just him. For the good and the bad, it was always the team. He wasn't a hero. And he wasn't a part of the team anymore.

"I told you from the beginning, I'm not doing that

damned event. I'm not a windup toy sailor to be paraded back and forth for someone else's ego."

She threw both hands in the air, giving him an exasperated look.

"This isn't about ego, Brody. It's about you accepting your due. It's about you being treated with the respect you deserve from a town that sucked at giving it to you before."

Respect?

For what?

If they knew the truth, everyone in town would see that he was the same loser they'd always judged him to be. The only one under any illusions was Genna.

"I'm not a damned hero. I'm just a guy trying to make a life here so we can be together. You don't want people to know you're dating a badass, that's your issue. If you don't know who I am, if you can't accept me for what I am, fine. But quit trying to make me into something I'm not to soothe your own ego."

The look of shocked misery on her face made Brody want to throw himself on an IED. Crap. He shoved both hands through his hair, totally at a loss. He didn't want to hurt Genna. But neither did he want to defend his decision. Because, as everyone in this room clearly knew, it was a lousy one. But he wasn't changing his mind. He wasn't fit to be a SEAL. And if he couldn't be a SEAL, he wasn't going to serve.

With that same sass he'd always admired, Genna took a deep breath and shook her head.

"The man I know, the man I've had a crush on since I was seventeen, the man I fell in love with? He's a hero. He's a badass with a miserable history. A man who overcame adversity, an abusive home and a knife in the gut to make something of himself. Something to be proud of. If that's not a hero, I don't know what is."

She sniffed, took a shaky breath, then shook her head

again as if she were trying to figure out where he'd gone wrong. "And now look at you. You're what? Throwing it all away because you are having identity issues. It's not because of me, Brody. Don't you dare pin this on *me*."

"Identity issues?" he sneered, wondering just how long she'd spent with Alexia. That shrink talk was apparently contagious.

"That's what I'd call it," she shot back. "You're either the guy who turns his back on his past to be a big bad SEAL, a hero with no ties to anyone or anything. Or you're the badass bad boy from the wrong side of town, the son of the drunk who lets the past limit his potential and shape his every decision."

Holy crap. Brody shook his head, wondering if Alexia had dropped off a psych profile to go with her contagious talk.

"You've got it all figured out?" he mused, anger wrapped around him so tight he felt that he was suffocating. "And, what? If I'd returned to the SEALs, or even to the navy, you'd have stood by me? Like you'd give up your golden life here as the pampered princess or walked away from your happy new business to live on base. For me? Yeah. Right."

For just a second, her chin trembled. Then she lifted it high and gave him an arch look.

"I guess we'll never know, will we? But for the record, yes. I'd have stood by you, whatever your decision. If you talked to me, and were honest about what you wanted, I'd have done anything for you. Stay here, hand out fliers for this lousy bar. Or follow you all over the world, waiting while you defended our country. I'd even built my happy new business around the idea of being portable, of doing it from anywhere. So I could be with you."

A single tear slid down her cheek, glistening in the dim light like a diamond.

"But then, you never asked. You decided to destroy your life instead." With that and an ugly look at the glass in his hand, she turned on her heel and sashayed out.

Not stormed or stomped. Nope, not Genna. She knew exactly how to hit him where it hurt, so she took her time, hips swinging and head held high.

Wrapped in bitterness, he watched her go. She shoved the door open, letting a blinding beam of sunshine into the bar before it slammed closed with a bang that ricocheted through the room. Leaving him in the dark.

Brody stared at the door for a long second.

Then, damning his entire life to hell, he tossed back the whiskey in a single gulp.

You'd think if a steady diet of cookies and sex was incredible, bingeing on just cookies to get over not having the sex would at least be okay.

Instead, it was rotten, sucky and miserable.

Genna stared at the pink polka-dotted fuzziness of her socks, one crossed over the other on the coffee table strewn with cookie crumbs, candy wrappers and an empty box of tissues.

What a cliché. Could she be any more pathetic? At least she hadn't given in to the urge to call friends to join her in the pity-fest.

Nope. This was not a side of herself she wanted to share. Or even admit.

As if on cue, her doorbell rang.

Genna sighed, shifting her feet off the coffee table and tucking them under her hip as she curled into a ball on the couch.

For three days, every time someone came to the door, she'd wiped her face, jumped up and run to see if it was Brody.

It never was.

Whoever it was this time, they'd go away.

"Genna? Can we talk?"

Unless they had their own key.

"I was worried about you."

Too tired to even get mad, she shifted her head but didn't lift it off the pillow.

"Not now, Dad."

"Your mom plans to come over this afternoon."

Genna sat up so fast her head spun. Blinking away the dizziness, she plastered on a cheerful look and brushed sugar off the knee of her sweatpants.

"I'm fine. Let Mom know you saw me and nothing is wrong. I was just taking a nap."

Standing in front of her now, her father scanned the littered table and gave a contemplative nod.

"Yeah. Those sugar crashes get ugly without a nap." Then, looking unsure for the first time Genna had ever seen, he offered a hesitant smile. "Or a hug from Dad?"

Her lips trembled and her eyes filled.

Before Genna could say yes or no, he was there. As he'd always been. With a hug and a strong shoulder. A solid wall she could depend on. Whether she wanted to or not.

He didn't say a word, though. No lecture. No *I told you so*'s. Just a hug.

Genna burst into tears.

He let her cry it out, grabbing napkins when he saw the tissue box was empty. He patted her back. He made sympathetic murmurs. She heard his teeth grinding at one point. But he didn't say a word.

Finally, whether because she was cried out or because she was worried keeping his opinion to himself was going to put her father into dentures, she pulled herself together.

"I yelled at Brody," she said quietly.

"Did he deserve to be yelled at?"

Genna frowned, peering through swollen eyes at the

man next to her. He looked like her father. He sounded like her father. He even smelled like him. But this was where her father would be offering up lectures and realigning her life to suit his vision.

Instead, he was watching her patiently. Waiting for her to respond.

Wow. Maybe they'd both grown up.

"I don't know if he deserved what I yelled," she confessed. "But I hated seeing him at Slims."

"What the hell were you doing at Slims? More to the point, what the hell is he doing there?" There he was, her normal father. His anger made her smile.

"Brody's working there."

"Why? He's got a job. He's a SEAL."

"He's quitting."

Genna waited.

But her father didn't explode. He didn't rant about losers and how he'd always been right. Instead he took a deep breath, which did nothing to clear away his frown, and nodded.

"That's why you yelled at him."

"Yep."

She waited for the interrogation. She saw a million questions in his eyes. But he said nothing. He just waited, letting her call the shots.

She wasn't sure she knew how. It was a little mind-boggling.

"You know, I've dreamed of him coming back for years," she said. "I never thought it'd really happen. It was one of those 'prince on a white steed sweeping in to save me from a life of blah' things."

"That's a lot to put on someone," her father said quietly. "As someone recently pointed out to me, we can't expect others to fill the empty places in our lives. That's something we have to figure out how to do on our own."

"I didn't have holes in my life," she said automatically. At her father's arch look, she sighed and shrugged. "Okay, so I wasn't happy. But it's not like I was sitting here stewing in misery, waiting for Brody to save me."

"Why did you wait until he was back to stand up for yourself and the things you really wanted then?"

Because it wasn't until she was with Brody again that she'd realized how much of herself she'd let go over the years. With him, she felt strong and clever and able to face any challenge. With him she felt safe. Like whatever happened, she could handle it.

Because he was her hero.

So instead of making him feel all those same things, she'd yelled at him, attacked his choices and all but called him a loser like his father. She'd tried to railroad him into doing what she thought was best, then had thrown a heavy dose of guilt on top of that just to make sure he got the message.

Her stomach churned. She swallowed hard to keep the cookies from making a reappearance.

Brody hadn't pushed her into her decisions. He hadn't nagged—granted, the idea of Brody Lane putting together enough words at one time to be considered nagging was strange. He'd just listened to her and let her figure it out for herself.

"I ruined everything," she said quietly, staring at her hands as if the reasons were written there somewhere. "I figured I knew what was best for him, and I tried to force him to do it, despite his own feelings."

"You had to get something from me besides your good looks," he said with a sympathetic expression.

Genna gave a shaky smile. Then she sighed.

"What do I do?"

For a second, her father's eyes lit with a controlling gleam. Then he banked it and shook his head.

"It wouldn't do me any good to tell you what to do, Genna. You need to figure it out yourself." He hesitated, then as if he couldn't resist, added, "Whatever it is, you need to make sure it's right for both of you. And that it's something you'll be comfortable living with for the rest of your life."

For the rest of her life?

Since she wanted to spend that with Brody, whatever it was, she'd better make it good.

14

"LANE."

Brody sighed, taking a second to rub at the pain knotted between his eyes before turning around. He set the case of beer he'd been carrying on the bar just in case he needed both hands.

"Sheriff."

"We need to talk."

"I'm still officially enlisted in the U.S. Navy on medical leave. If you're looking to drive me out of town, you're going to need a new game plan."

Reilly offered a chilly look, then gave a quick nod.

"Good to know."

"You might also want to know that I'm not playing this time," Brody said, figuring he might as well lay it all out from the get-go. "You have an issue, you deal with me direct and we hash it out. You're not calling the shots, but I'm willing to work with you to make Genna's life easier."

Reilly's stare grew contemplative.

"Actually it's Genna I'm here to talk about."

"I figured."

"My daughter isn't happy. I accept my share of the

blame and I'm working on that. I figure you need to step up, too, and deal with yours."

Sheriff Reilly wanted him to fix things with his little princess? Brody tensed. That, he hadn't figured.

"Isn't this why Genna stopped talking to you?"

"There's a difference between looking out for someone, in trying to help make their life a little smoother, and in trying to force them to live their lives the way you want."

"So wouldn't your being here fall under the forcing things category?" Brody asked. Even when he wasn't trying to run his daughter's life, the guy still had to poke his nose in?

"I don't see that I'm forcing anything. Just having a conversation."

"Nice." Brody rolled his eyes.

"Genna said you're leaving the navy. Why?"

"Why the hell do people keep asking me that?" Brody shoved his hand through his hair, even more irritated to feel how long it'd grown since he'd been on leave. Just another sign that he didn't fit, wasn't himself. "I'm getting out. End of discussion. I thought that'd make Genna happy. Don't women want guys who are around more than a few months a year?"

"I can't claim to be an expert on women, but I think they'd want a guy who's honest with them. One who lives his purpose, even if that purpose doesn't revolve around them. If you leave the service because you think it's what she wants or because you think that's the only way you can make a relationship work, then your odds of going the distance are pretty slim. She's either strong enough to handle your career, or she's not. Don't put the burden of her happiness on your shoulders."

"Quite a statement from a dad who spent the last ten years putting that burden on his daughter."

Cheap shot, but Brody was feeling mean.

The sheriff took it like a man, though. Instead of snapping back, he simply nodded. Leaving Brody to feel like an ass.

"I won't be getting any parenting awards. In retrospect, I'm pretty sure Cara and I made every mistake in the book. And our children paid for them." Reilly paused, clenching his jaw and his face tight with grief. "Genna and Joe paid for our mistakes. The same as you paid for Brian's."

"Not even close to the same thing." Shaking his head, Brody grimaced. "Whatever mistakes you made, and I'm not saying there weren't some head scratchers, you always loved your kids. You acted out of concern. They knew that. Both of them."

He didn't bother to add that Brian hadn't had an ounce of love to offer anyone, let alone his son. And his only concern had always been himself.

"I'll deny it if you ever repeat this," Brody said quietly, feeling like an idiot but scanning the empty room anyway to make sure he wasn't overheard. "But I used to be jealous of Joe having a guy like you for a dad. I always figured if I had kids, I'd do a lot of things the way you did. Not all of them, since I'm a fan of learning from other people's screwups. But some."

"Thank you," Reilly said quietly. His face wasn't any less tight, but he'd lost that miserable look in his eyes. "I guess it's only fair that I tell you that there weren't a few times after you shipped out that I didn't wish Joe were more like you."

Holy crap. Brody jerked his shoulders, trying to shake off the emotional impact of that. This was getting ridiculous. A few more exchanges like that and they'd be hugging and offering to do each other's fingernails.

Still, he knew what it must have cost the guy to say that, so he could only offer honesty in return.

"I'm not leaving the navy because of Genna."

The sheriff arched one brow and waited.

Brody ground his teeth. This definitely wasn't one of those "jealous for Reilly as a father" moments.

"I failed. You know how that goes, right? Despite any random thoughts you might have had to the contrary, you've called it plenty of times when you said I was a loser."

The sheriff rocked back on his heels, both hands in his front pockets as he considered that.

"You're talking about the guy who was killed on this mission?"

Brody went hot, then cold. Fury iced in his veins, freezing out his regret over how things had gone down with Genna. What the hell? She'd shared what he'd told her? Fists clenched, he wondered if the bar would withstand a few solid punches. As the fury coiled tighter, he realized he didn't care.

Before he could release his anger on the decrepit wood, the sheriff held up one hand.

"The mayor pulled strings, called in a few favors to get the basics for the hero event he put together. Nothing classified, all approved by your admiral."

Tension seeping away, Brody wondered how many different ways he could feel like an ass in one conversation.

"I figure that kind of thing, losing someone like that, it might give you second thoughts. Inspire a little worry. Maybe even fear."

"I'm not afraid," Brody said dismissively. Shaking his head at that crazy thought, he laughed and went back to stacking cases of beer. Time to call an end to this conversation.

"Not for yourself."

Brody froze. He took a deep breath, slowly lowering the box onto the bar. Okay then. The conversation wasn't quite over.

He gave the older man a questioning look.

"No? Then who am I afraid for?"

"Only you can answer that." The sheriff shrugged. "If it were me, though, I'd probably be worried about my teammates. Maybe a little concerned that I couldn't pull off the mission perfectly, so that means I was flawed. That I wasn't a solid SEAL."

Brody had taken plenty of hits in his day. Some he'd been braced for, others had come as a complete shock. But nothing had knocked him on his ass quite like the sheriff's words.

He had to take a few breaths to pull his thoughts together. A few more to shake off the creepy feeling that the other guy was peeking through his brain for information.

"Your teammates are SEALs," he finally said, matching Reilly's light, conversational tone. "They're trained to kick ass and if they thought you were afraid for them, they'd kick yours."

The sheriff's lips twitched.

"And the rest?"

Brody shrugged. The rest was right on target. But he wasn't a pansy-ass. He'd spent most of his life being called a loser, feeling like his situation flawed him in one way or another. He'd overcome it before, he could overcome it again.

"You know, I was a green rookie right out of the police academy when I married Genna's mother. I was so damned cocky, so sure I could handle anything." Reilly smiled, a reminiscing look on his face. "Then I got a domestic abuse call. Before I could knock on the door, the guy shot me."

Brody frowned. Obviously it hadn't been fatal. But still…

"My first thought as I hit the ground was Cara. That she was going to freak, want me to quit the force. My second thought was that it hurt like a son of a bitch, and that

I wasn't as invincible as I'd figured." The man paused, whether reliving the moment or for effect to let those words sink in, Brody wasn't sure. "But Cara didn't freak. She never asked me to quit, and if she worried, she never let on. And you know what? Not being invincible made me a better cop."

If he'd taken a huge stick and smacked Brody upside the head with it, the guy couldn't have hammered the message home any stronger.

It wasn't just his own fears Brody had been nursing like a dirty little secret. He'd generously assigned a whole slew of them to Genna, too. Fears she'd never once voiced, probably hadn't even considered.

But worrying about her fears, protecting her at his own expense? That'd been a hell of a lot easier than admitting his own.

Brody dropped his head back, staring at the ceiling and trying to figure out how he'd lost sight of the simple facts.

Genna was sweet, loving and sassy. She was clever, gorgeous and talented. And she was strong. Strong enough to tell him what she wanted. And what she didn't want.

But he hadn't given her a chance.

He'd done the same thing he'd cussed her father out for.

He'd made the decisions for her, all in the name of protecting her.

Maybe he was more like the good sheriff than any of them realized. And that wasn't necessarily a good thing.

"Figure it out?" Reilly asked after giving Brody a few minutes to stew in his own stupidity.

"I blew it," Brody confessed. Then he shrugged and shook his head. "I'm surprised she didn't kick my ass before she walked out."

"You want to make it up to her?"

No. He'd rather find her, kiss her crazy until she forgot all the stupidity of the last week, then lose himself in her body for a few hours. But he didn't figure that was the answer. Nor anything her father needed to know.

So he shrugged instead.

"Tucker went ahead with that event. The hero thing? It's happening in about, oh—" he checked his watch "—ten minutes."

"Without me?"

"Our esteemed mayor doesn't like to waste a chance to show off for the press."

Damn.

The only thing Brody wanted less than facing the crappy thoughts tangled up in his head was to stand up in front of a bunch of people and be declared a freaking hero. He wasn't one.

But Genna saw him as one.

Which, he finally let himself admit, made him feel pretty damned good.

Besides, if he went it'd make her happy.

And he wanted that more than he wanted to hide.

"I'm not saying I changed my mind," he declared, grabbing the bar keys from under the counter, then snagging his jacket. "I'm doing this for Genna. So she knows I'm not a total ass."

And, maybe, so she'd forgive him.

Then he could get rid of this sick feeling in his gut. And maybe, just maybe, they could talk about the future and how she'd feel about sharing hers with a SEAL.

Maybe.

If he changed his mind.

Following Reilly to the cop car, Brody realized that while he'd ridden in a few over the years, this was his first visit to the front seat. Then the sheriff hit the road.

"Where are we going? Town hall is the other way."

"We gotta stop by your place. Your gramma made arrangements for your dress uniform to be here in case you decided to do her proud today."

Dress whites?

Shit.

A HALF HOUR LATER, Brody flexed his shoulders to try to get the heavy fabric of his uniform to lie comfortably. His hat tucked under his arm, he took a second to glare at the spit-shine polish on his black shoes and wonder if his gramma had done that. Then another moment to absorb how special it was that she had.

"C'mon," Reilly said quietly.

Since the cop had parked illegally in front of the town hall, all they had to do was mount the steps and push through the wide doors. All the way, Brody focused as if he was approaching a mission. No room for emotions. He was here to do a job. A job that he was trained for, one that his military résumé claimed he was qualified to do.

A deep breath, his emotions locked tight in some far corner he never saw when he was in the zone, he entered the battle—or as everyone else called it, the main hall.

And stopped short.

Damn, this was bigger than he'd expected. It looked as though the entire town had crowded into the huge room. Off to one side were a handful of strangers, cameras and recorders in hand. The press. On stage the mayor stood at a lectern, Genna seated to his right. To the left was a row of chairs, all but one filled.

His team. To a man, they were all here. Like him, they were all decked out in dress whites. He tensed, his eyes widening when he saw who was seated in the command position. Admiral Pierce? Wasn't it bad enough being declared a hero in front of a team of men just as heroic? But they'd brought in the brass, too?

Then he noticed the large framed photo propped before the podium.

Carter.

This wasn't about him, Brody realized.

This event was to honor Carter.

The real hero.

Reeling with emotions so strong they almost knocked him on his ass, Brody's gaze cut to Genna. She stared right back, her chin high and pride in her eyes. She'd arranged this. She'd understood what he hadn't.

His gut ached with the power of his feelings.

He looked at his team.

And knew they were all feeling the same thing.

Pride and loss.

Knowing, accepting, that he belonged up there next to them, Brody nodded to Reilly, then made his way to the front of the room. After his salute to the admiral, he took his seat.

"Ladies and gentlemen, thank you for joining us today," the mayor said, his tone holding jovial respect. "I'd like to offer a special thanks to our honored guests. Admiral Pierce, Bedford's own Brody Lane, as well as the United States Navy SEAL team he serves with."

Mayor Tucker dived into his speech with gusto, reveling in the attention but keeping a sober, respectful tone that made it clear that this was more than just a promo op for him.

After he wound up his words by expressing pride that the town could call one of their own a part of such an esteemed group, he handed the lectern over to the SEALs.

Brody joined his team as they honored their fallen comrade. Like the others, when his time came he stood and said a few words. Not about heroism, or about his own loss. He spoke of what it meant to be a SEAL. Of why they did what they did. It wasn't for glory, or even for ac-

knowledgment. That's why their missions were classified.
They did it because they were the best. Because they were
the ones who could.

As he finished, he looked at his team. Landon, Masters, Castillo and the rest. Their faces echoed the pride he
felt. By the time he stepped away from the lectern, he'd
found peace.

His gaze found Genna's.

And there, he'd found love.

He figured it was a lucky man who could claim both.
And an idiot who'd let either go.

GENNA WIPED THE tears from her cheeks, but they just kept
coming. Thankfully, nobody was looking at her as she
moved off the stage. All eyes were on the SEALs as the
men stood to leave. She wouldn't have been surprised if
the building didn't tilt to one side, everyone moved toward
them so quickly.

"Genna."

After another quick swipe over her cheeks, she turned
to offer the mayor a smile.

"That was fabulous. Wonderful," he gushed, almost
bouncing in his Gucci loafers he was so excited. "I wasn't
sure about the changes at first, but you were so right.
Kudos. If you ever want a job with me again, it's yours."

After a quick pat on her shoulder, he made like a whirl-
wind toward the press. Leaving Genna to blink. Wow. The
man had never been that effusive when he'd actually had
to sign her paycheck.

"Nice offer."

Sighing, she turned to face her parents. "I'm not going
back to work for the mayor."

"Of course you're not, darling," her mother said, elbow-
ing her husband. "I've been playing hostess at the dessert

table. Sweetheart, your offerings are amazing. And the money people are paying!"

Genna and her father exchanged smiles. Nothing turned Cara Reilly's opinion around faster than other people's opinions. Especially when those opinions were made in cash.

"I just wanted to sneak away for a moment to give you a kiss and tell you how proud I am," her mother continued. "Now I'm going back to the table. I want to make sure every sale includes a flier for your business. I'm keeping a list, too, of people who've expressed interest. I'll be happy to follow up and remind them to buy stuff later."

As excited as if she'd thought it up and pushed Genna into starting Sugar and Spice herself, Cara gave her daughter a quick kiss, then hurried off.

"Thank you," she said quietly to her father.

"I didn't change her mind," he said with a shrug. "And I'm still not completely sure this is a good idea. There are a lot of risks. But I do believe you can handle them."

"Then thank you twice," Genna said with a reluctant laugh. "For believing I can handle myself. And for bringing Brody."

Her dad nodded, his gaze cutting across the room. Maybe it was the white uniforms, or just the general air of command, but the SEALs stood out as if a spotlight were shining on them.

"He's a good man," her father told her. He offered a bittersweet smile. "The kind of man anyone would be proud to have for a son."

Oh. Genna had thought she was through with tears. Knowing how hard that was for her father to say, to even think given his guilt and anger over Joe, all she could do was offer a hug. And sniffle a little more.

"Go on," her dad said after giving her a quick squeeze. "You have things to do."

"No." She looked around the room, so glad she wasn't ever going to have to plan one of these things again. "My part is done."

"That's not what I meant."

Genna looked toward the podium, her eyes immediately finding Brody. She'd done this for him. To honor what she thought he believed heroism to be. To give everyone, including herself, a chance to show their gratitude for what he and others like him did. And, maybe, to give him a little closure.

She hadn't thought about after, though.

And now that it was here, she was nervous.

"Maybe later. This is his moment. I'll talk to him after the crowd disperses." Or at his gramma's. Or maybe she'd write a letter.

"Excuse me."

"Or you could try now." With an inclination of his head and a twitch of his lips, her father gave Genna an arch look and said, "Good luck." And left.

Just like that. Years of overprotective hovering and he chose this moment to let her sink or swim?

Her nerves jangling so hard in her system, she was surprised her entire body wasn't vibrating, Genna pressed her lips together, took a breath and turned around.

Oh. He was so gorgeous.

She'd never been one of those women who swooned over a guy in uniform before. But Brody in uniform? Delicious.

"Can we talk?" he asked quietly.

She wasn't sure she was ready to. She'd been so nasty to him before, then instead of trying to fix things, she'd arranged an event he'd specifically said he didn't want.

"Seriously? *You* want to talk?" she asked, trying to sound as if she was teasing instead of nervous. She gestured to the group of still-surrounded men. "It looks like the admiral is leaving—shouldn't you say goodbye? Why don't you spend this time with your friends? I'll be here if you want to talk later."

Here, home, somewhere.

But Brody didn't even look around. Instead, those golden eyes stared, intense and hypnotic. Genna wanted to squirm. Not from nerves this time, though. Nope, that was pure sexual heat in that gaze. The kind that made her want to strip him out of that delicious uniform and taste everything underneath.

"C'mon," he said, taking her hand. Fingers wrapped around hers, he led her to the door. "I can talk to them later. We need to talk now."

Later?

Unlike Brody, Genna looked back. She caught Blake's eye. The other man, admittedly dashing in his uniform, gave her a slow nod. For the success of the event? Or because he thought Brody might be returning to his team? Blake's expression didn't give anything away. Damn, these men were hard to read.

Still, she didn't ask. Not while Brody led her out of the building. Not when he looked around, then guided her over to the small gazebo across the street from the town hall. Not when he took off his hat, tossed it on the bench and took her hands.

She did melt a little then, though. It felt so good to touch him again. It wasn't until this second that she realized how afraid she'd been that she'd never be able to again.

"I'm sorry," she said quickly, before he could say a word.

"What for?"

"For yelling at you. For trying to push you into doing what I thought was best. For going ahead with this event, knowing your feelings about it."

"For thinking I was a hero?"

"Hardly." Genna gave him an *are you kidding* look. "If you don't want to see yourself that way, that's fine. I mean, who wants a guy who thinks he's so awesome he should be declared a hero?"

"Say what?" Looking confused, Brody shook his head as if trying to clear his ears. "I thought you thought..."

"That I thought you were a hero?" she finished when his words trailed away. At his sheepish nod, she pulled both hands out of his to frame his face. Staring into his eyes, she smiled. "I don't think you're a hero. I know you are. You're my hero. Whatever else you do, whether it's saving the world or pouring whiskey, you'll be my hero. Because you saved me. From myself, from my fears, from wasting my life."

He started to shake his head, so she hurried on before he could interrupt.

"You helped me realize that I have to stand up for myself. And that even if it isn't welcome, that sometimes we have to stand up for others."

She waited to see if he understood that she didn't blame him for trying to protect her. Again. When he tilted his chin, she knew he did.

"I'm strong enough to build my own life, Brody. To make it with you, while you're by my side. Or while you're away, serving our country. I'm even strong enough to survive without you." She had to stop and swallow the tears that threatened to choke her words. "You're my hero. And I'm strong enough to be yours."

For a brief moment, Brody looked so vulnerable. His gaze was soft and his smile sweet. He leaned down, resting his forehead on hers, and closed his eyes. A heartbeat later, he brushed a gentle kiss over her lips.

"I love you," he whispered. "Forever. I think I've loved you forever."

Too happy even for tears, Genna offered an ecstatic smile. She brushed her fingers over his cheeks, then sighed.

"I love you, too. Just as much, and for just as long. You really are my hero, Brody. You always will be."

"Lane."

Brody held Genna's gaze for a long, heart-melting second longer. Then, transforming before her eyes, he came to attention, did an about-face and saluted.

"Sir."

"Report for duty Monday morning at oh-six-hundred."

Genna pressed her fingers to her lips, trying not to cry. She'd never thought she'd be so happy to hear that the man she loved was committing to spend a huge amount of time away from her. But she'd never thought she'd love someone like Brody, either.

"Yes, sir."

His face blank, Blake returned the salute. Then he flashed Genna a quick smile and a wink before rejoining his grinning wife.

Brody waited until they were out of earshot before turning back to take Genna's hands.

"So. I have to go back to work," he said quietly. He brought one hand, then the other, to his lips to brush each with a soft kiss. "For the next month, at least, I'll be based in Coronado. I can put in a request for military housing instead of the barracks. Or I can come back here and visit on weekends for a while. Until you decide what you want to do."

"What do you want me to do?"

"Whatever makes you happy."

"You," she said simply. "You make me happy."

And there it was.

Genna was smart enough to recognize happy ever after when she was staring right at it. And wise enough to know that while it wasn't always going to be easy, her life with Brody was going to be amazing.

Her lips met his, their kiss as sweet as their declarations.

They were going to live happily ever after.

* * * * *

#787 CAPTIVATE ME
Unrated!
by Kira Sinclair

What is it about Mardi Gras that makes everyone lose their mind? When Alyssa Vaughn notices a masked stranger watching her undress through her bedroom window, the Bacchus attitude takes over. But wait until she finds out who he is!

#788 TEXAS OUTLAWS: COLE
The Texas Outlaws
by Kimberly Raye

Cole Chisholm's love life is even wilder than the horses he rides. When Nikki Barbie asks him to pretend to be her boyfriend, he agrees...but only if some wild, wicked nights are included!

#789 ALONE WITH YOU
Made in Montana
by Debbi Rawlins

Alexis Worthington is smart, ambitious and has a wild streak that alienated her from her family. Now's her chance to prove herself to them. But working with rodeo rider Will Tanner—she's finding it difficult to behave!

#790 UNEXPECTED TEMPTATION
The Berringers
by Samantha Hunter

Luke Berringer thinks he's finally put his past to rest when he catches the woman who ruined his life—but in Vanessa Grant has he actually found the woman who will heal his heart?

HBCNM0214

REQUEST YOUR FREE BOOKS!
2 FREE NOVELS PLUS 2 FREE GIFTS!

red-hot reads!

YES! Please send me 2 FREE Harlequin® Blaze™ novels and my 2 FREE gifts (gifts are worth about $10). After receiving them, if I don't wish to receive any more books, I can return the shipping statement marked "cancel." If I don't cancel, I will receive 4 brand-new novels every month and be billed just $4.74 per book in the U.S. or $4.96 per book in Canada. That's a savings of at least 14% off the cover price. It's quite a bargain. Shipping and handling is just 50¢ per book in the U.S. and 75¢ per book in Canada.* I understand that accepting the 2 free books and gifts places me under no obligation to buy anything. I can always return a shipment and cancel at any time. Even if I never buy another book, the two free books and gifts are mine to keep forever.

150/350 HDN F4WC

Name _____ (PLEASE PRINT) _____

Address _____ Apt. # _____

City _____ State/Prov. _____ Zip/Postal Code _____

Signature (if under 18, a parent or guardian must sign) _____

Mail to the **Harlequin® Reader Service:**
IN U.S.A.: P.O. Box 1867, Buffalo, NY 14240-1867
IN CANADA: P.O. Box 609, Fort Erie, Ontario L2A 5X3

**Want to try two free books from another line?
Call 1-800-873-8635 or visit www.ReaderService.com.**

* Terms and prices subject to change without notice. Prices do not include applicable taxes. Sales tax applicable in N.Y. Canadian residents will be charged applicable taxes. Offer not valid in Quebec. This offer is limited to one order per household. Not valid for current subscribers to Harlequin Blaze books. All orders subject to credit approval. Credit or debit balances in a customer's account(s) may be offset by any other outstanding balance owed by or to the customer. Please allow 4 to 6 weeks for delivery. Offer available while quantities last.

Your Privacy—The Harlequin® Reader Service is committed to protecting your privacy. Our Privacy Policy is available online at www.ReaderService.com or upon request from the Harlequin Reader Service.

We make a portion of our mailing list available to reputable third parties that offer products we believe may interest you. If you prefer that we not exchange your name with third parties, or if you wish to clarify or modify your communication preferences, please visit us at www.ReaderService.com/consumerchoice or write to us at Harlequin Reader Service Preference Service, P.O. Box 9062, Buffalo, NY 14269. Include your complete name and address.

Amid the revelry of Mardi Gras, Beckett Kayne just wanted a
moment of peace. He was enjoying the solitude when a light
snapped on in the apartment across the alley.

She stood, framed by the window. A soft radiance lit her
from behind, painting her in an ethereal splash of color that
made her seem dreamy and tragic and somehow unreal.

Maybe that was why he kept watching. Logically, he realized he was intruding, but there was something about her....

Her eyelids slid closed and her head tipped back. Exhaustion was stamped into every line of her body, but that didn't
detract from her allure. In fact, it made Beckett want to reach
out and hold her. To take her weight and the exhaustion on
himself.

Her hands drifted slowly up her body, settling at the top
button of her blouse. With sure fingers, she popped it open.
And another. And another. The edge of her red-hot bra came
into view revealing an enticing swell of skin.

Tension snapped through Beckett's body. The hedonistic pressure of the night must have gotten to him, after all. Because, even as his brain was screaming at him to give her privacy, he couldn't do it.

It had been a very long time since any woman had pulled this kind of immediate physical reaction from him.

Perhaps it was the air of innocence not even the windowpane and ten feet of alley could camouflage. She was simply herself—unconsciously sensual.

Shifting, Beckett dropped his foot and settled his waist against the edge of the balcony railing. He wanted to be the one uncovering her soft skin. Running his fingers over her body. Hearing the hitch of her breath when he discovered a sensitive spot.

Maybe it was his movement that caught her attention. Suddenly her head snapped sideways and she looked straight into his eyes.

Her fingers stilled. Surprise, embarrassment and anger flitted across her face before finally settling into something darker and a hell of a lot more sinful.

Her arms stretched wide. She undulated, rolling her hips and ribs and spine in a way that begged him to touch.

And then the blinds snapped down between them.

Pick up CAPTIVATE ME by Kira Sinclair, available in March 2014 wherever you buy Harlequin® Blaze® books.

Get ready for a wild ride!

Cole Chisholm's love life is even wilder than the horses he rides. When Nikki Barbie asks him to pretend to be her boyfriend, he agrees...but only if some wild, wicked nights are included.

Pick up the final chapter of
The Texas Outlaws miniseries

Texas Outlaws: Cole

by *USA TODAY* bestselling author

Kimberly Raye

AVAILABLE FEBRUARY 18, 2014,
wherever you buy Harlequin Blaze books.

HB79792

Rules are made to be broken!

Alexis Worthington is smart, ambitious and has a wild streak that alienated her from her family. Now's her chance to prove herself to them. But working with rodeo rider Will Tanner—she's finding it difficult to behave!

Don't miss

Alone with You

by reader-favorite author

Debbi Rawlins

AVAILABLE FEBRUARY 18, 2014, wherever you buy Harlequin Blaze books.

Love the Harlequin book you just read?

Your opinion matters.

Review this book on your favorite book site, review site, blog or your own social media properties and share your opinion with other readers!